A Deafening Whisper

Music of the Soul - Volume 2

By Erik Schubach

Self publishing

P.O. Box 523

Nine Mile Falls, WA 99026

Manufactured in the United States of America

FIRST EDITION

ISBN 978-1484192993

Prologue

Mia Jacobs was busy in the art studio in her garage, putting the finishing touches on the two pieces for the Christmas exhibit at the downtown Seattle gallery. She had turned down four other prestigious galleries across the nation for this exhibit. After all, it was only right to show it in their hometown. It still amazed her that her art was in such high demand. To her, it was just her imperfect way of conveying her own feelings and emotions, and she never thought that anyone else would understand what she was trying to say with each piece.

She was frowning, not a good look for her attractive face that just screamed femininity, it caused little crows feet to appear at the side of her eyes. That's something she was noticing lately as she rapidly approached her fortieth birthday, little lines like that appeared more and more frequently. Though she looked almost ten years younger, she still felt old unless she was working on her art or speaking with her daughter.

Mia was never satisfied with her own work, especially when the subject was the love of her life. It had to be perfect, for... her. Mia's obsessive compulsive nature had her assessing each piece over and over again, checking and rechecking everything from the composition to the alignment of each individual component.

She brushed the straight, raven-black hair that had fallen forward as she worked back over her shoulder. It was annoyingly long, but that's the way her wife liked it.

This grouping was a series of collages on two huge canvases. Hundreds of tiny photographs of her wife assembled in a manner that, from a given distance, formed a portrait of the woman she loved. Inset into each collage was a series darker photos that formed words across the large canvases, celebrating works of poetry by her wife.

To most people, it was shocking that she could see the tints of each photo in her head and arrange them like pixels on a computer screen to form larger images that were almost picture perfect at a distance. But to her, it was just how her brain worked. She never had to back up to see the result, she knew exactly what it looked like. She used to think that things like that meant that her mind was broken or defective until she met her bride.

The final photograph was put in place and she dabbed decoupage paste across it, sealing it in place. Seven strokes left, seven strokes right, seven strokes up, seven strokes down. “Damn,” she muttered as she saw her last down-stoke had a tiny clump no bigger than the head of a pin. Nobody would ever have seen it in a million years, especially since the decoupage would dry clear, but she would obsess over it.

So she quickly walked, counting seconds in her head, over to the deep metal utility sink beside the door that led into the house, and washed the paste from her brush. Then she returned to her bench and placed the brush, neatly parallel to her other brushes, being sure to align the bottom of the brush with the bottoms of the others. She nudged it slightly up and down until it was correctly aligned.

She then turned to her other tools and retrieved a small scraper, with a flat tip no bigger than a pencil and meticulously removed the clump from her art. Then she rushed over to sink again, the countdown in her head continuing, to wash the scraper then return it to its place beside the other tools. Nudging it until it was properly positioned.

She took a breath, knowing she was doing the obsessive compulsive thing that just drove her wife crazy. Not the bad kind of crazy, but the "that's so hot" kind of crazy. This brought a small smile to her lips. She was the only person that had ever fully embraced Mia's quirks and made her feel normal.

She sighed and grabbed her brush again, dipping it into the decoupage and started over on the last photo. Seven strokes left, seven strokes right, seven strokes up, seven strokes down. Mia exhaled the breath she didn't know she was holding. Then she turned and walked to the sink again to wash the brush, and then replaced it with the other brushes, making sure it was placed just right.

She looked at the small worn out white teddy bear on the workbench as she sealed the jar of paste, the one with its tattered pink bow and holding a little heart. Then she placed the container in its proper place on the workbench, turning it so that the label was exactly parallel to the edge of the work surface. As she motioned over to the canvases she grinned at the stuffed animal and asked, “So what do you think Little Vee?”

She took off her smock and hung it on the wall hook next to the bench, smoothing out any wrinkles. She then swept her emerald gaze around the spotless, almost sterile garage/studio to make sure everything was in its proper place. She looked at all the artwork hung on the walls, her wife's large leather bound books of handwritten poems on their shelf, and an almost antique FJ Cruiser in pristine condition in the far bay before being satisfied.

The door into the house opened just as the countdown in her head expired and she reached over to snatch her three-inch tall teddy bear from the counter. She turned to the door as she idly stuffed Little Vee into the pocket of her relaxed jeans. The same spot the little bear has lived the past twenty-two years.

Mia smiled as her daughter Abbey laughingly bounded through the door, dragging her girlfriend, Sam with her. They were holding hands with their fingers interlaced. Mia couldn't help but smile wider, remembering how she and her wife had been almost inseparable like that as well, always needing the touch of the other. Abbey flashed a toothy white smile at her mother.

“It is exactly 6:00 on the dot ma, just like you requested. I take it you finished on time?”

Mia could tell Abbey was trying hard not to laugh at her own inside joke, knowing that clocks were jealous of her mother's internal timer. Mia just rolled her eyes. “Well, by coincidence, I just happened to finish a moment ago.” She motioned over at the canvases. The girls looked over, admiring her work.

It never ceased to amaze Mia how Abbey looked so strikingly like her mother with her mane of curly brown locks flowing over her shoulder and her stunning amber eyes, so light they looked almost orange, giving her a catlike quality. Her tall, thin frame conveying feminine grace, the girl next door look of her face fit her friendly outgoing personality to a T. She liked everyone, and it was almost impossible not to like her too. Her smile was so infectious.

Mia turned her attention to Samantha as the girl was looking at the artwork. She had to hand it to her daughter, she really knew how to pick them, this girl, for lack of a better word, was gorgeous. At first glance, you would believe she was a model. With her layered straight blonde hair and its single signature curly pink shock on the left side that brought your eyes to her face. Her complexion was perfect without needing much makeup. What little makeup she did wear drew your gaze to her radiant, ice blue eyes that sparkled with a great deal of intelligence and emotion.

She surely had curves in all the right places, which she showed off easily with the clothes she wore. Today she was in a pair of jeans that were so tight they could have been a second skin. The short white and pink tank tee showed just enough of her toned stomach and abs to make even a preacher blush. All of this just screamed "Barbie" to Mia the first time she met Sam when Abbey had brought her home one weekend in her freshman year at the New York Academy of Art.

That first impression was quickly thrown out when they all sat around and spoke seriously that first night. Samantha was intelligent, witty, caring, and very protective of Abbey and her feelings. This won Mia over quickly, and she has viewed Sam as a second daughter these past four years. None of the other boyfriends or girlfriends that Abbey had ever dated had been able to accomplish this.

As Abbey smirked at her mother, quipping, "Oh, a coincidence is it?"

Sam had her head tilted, really absorbing the canvases in the middle of the garage. She spoke quietly in her rich British accent, "I know those poems. We read them in our contemporary American Literature class. They're by Vee A. Jacobs." Her eyes narrowed and she looked back and forth between the canvases and the two other women.

Realization hit her and she looked at them accusingly, then spoke to Abbey, "Oh my God! Not only is your mother Mia friggin' Jacobs, but your other mom is Vee Jacobs?!? Why didn't either of you ever tell me?"

Mia noticed Abbey bite her lower lip in want at the sound of Sam's accent. She smiled to herself, recognizing the look.

Sam looked at the first canvas with the profile of a beautiful woman that reminded her of Abbey, but she knew the woman was Abbey's other mom, she had seen old photos. The darker pictures formed words, with letters crisp enough at this distance to look like a perfectly formed font.

Every Day
A gift.
A breath.
A look.

A touch.
A smile.
A love.

Fleeting glances. A stolen kiss.
Your loving embrace.
Teardrops fall. A granted wish.

The words resonated with Sam, they felt like the way she thought of Abbey, like how their relationship began four years ago. She shook her head and turned to the other canvas. It held another poem by Vee Jacobs with that same woman holding a baby. She heard Abbey chuckle as she spoke, "Well, it kinda never came up. I keep forgetting that my parents are famous, I just see them as, well, just my moms. I told you she dabbled in poetry." She shot one of her patent pending, knee buckling innocent smiles at Sam.

Counting
Two hearts.
One soul.

Two minds.
One thought.

Two voices.
One love.

A single lingering touch.
Merging.
A deafening whisper.

Sam snorted. "Dabbled?" This one was Sam's favorite, that last line "A deafening whisper," struck her as so profound and powerful without even knowing why. She smiled and turned back to the two women shaking her head in disbelief.

Mia just grinned and grabbed both of their hands and dragged them into the house. "Come along ladies, let's catch up a bit before I start dinner. I only get you two for the holidays before that dreadful school steals you away from me again. Thank God you two graduate this year."

Abbey and Sam laughed as they were dragged through the kitchen, past the huge Christmas tree, and to the living room and the super comfy couch. Mia jumped up cross-legged onto one side of the couch as the two girls snuggled into each other beside her. The older woman grabbed a little remote off the side table and started some soft violin Christmas music in the background for some ambiance. Then placed the remote back in its place, nudging it around until it was exactly perpendicular to the edge of the table.

The girls waited patiently for her to finish. "So tell me about school. I haven't heard much out of you girls since spring break," Mia said with an eager twinkle in her eyes. She loved her daughter more than anything and was fascinated with anything about her. She was still amazed that she had come from her. She was so glad Abbey had found someone to make her happy. A blind man could see how the two young ladies felt for each other.

Abbey spoke up, "Well actually mother, can we do that a little later. There's a story I want you to share with Sammie first if that's okay. It is pretty important. Could you tell her the story about how you and mom met? It's pretty epic." Abbey's eyes were twinkling as she grabbed Sam's hand and laced their fingers together, feeling her warmth.

Mia smiled softly, settling deeper into the couch for the story, already getting lost in the memory. "I never get tired of sharing the story of my Valla and me." She looked over at the two girls and smiled fondly at them as she began.

Chapter 1 - Define Yourself

First let me tell you a little bit about myself. I was a pretty shy kid growing up. I had a couple quirks, but they were pretty manageable. I used to stutter a bit whenever I got nervous, it still pops up from time to time. Also, I've always been a little obsessive compulsive, but not to a debilitating degree. The doctors always said it was usually indicative of a larger problem, and boy did that wind up being the understatement of the century right around the time I hit puberty.

That's when the symptoms of my condition started manifesting themselves with a vengeance. The first time it struck was in the seventh grade. I was stressing about a math test I was about to take, even though math comes as easy to me as breathing, when my shoulder suddenly twitched up, brushing my cheek. I thought it was odd, but then it happened again, and again. I started to get scared and raised my hand to get the teacher's attention as it continued. I was going to say something when I blurted out, “It's my pencil!”

I was on the verge of panic. Am I having a stroke or something? Aren't I too young for that? As these thoughts passed through my head, I again blurted out, “It's my pencil, not yours!” I continued to twitch and rambled things about my pencil. The class was laughing and the teacher, Mrs. McGinniss, ran to my side with a look of distress on her face. I was crying and just wanted to melt away.
“My pencil.”

The twitching stopped as I was being led away to the nurse's office. My foster parents brought me to the doctor, who couldn't find anything wrong. Over the next couple weeks, another episode, a bunch of tests and more doctor's visits it was determined that I had Tourette Syndrome. But the doctors said that in most cases the symptoms would clear up as I matured into adulthood.

Fat lot of good that did me at that time, my classmates had already started the teasing that would follow me the rest of my school years. “Freak” and “Spaz” were the common nicknames that were applied to me and everyone avoided me like the plague. The ones that didn't avoid me usually pushed me around or tripped me in the halls to make me look like more of a freak.

I had retreated within myself, trying to hide and to not be noticed. I started wearing dark hoodies with the hood up at all times, the sleeves pulled over my hands. I just wanted to disappear. School was a living hell for me. I'd take sack lunches and hide outside or in the back halls to eat. I rarely spoke with anyone and just focused on my schoolwork and art. Art was a good release for me, it felt like math, and my obsessive nature virtually guaranteed my 4.0 average in my other classes.

High school wound up being ten times worse than junior high, the symptoms got worse and the episodes increased in frequency. They were brought on mostly by stress from the harassment other students subjected me to. The only semi-positive thing was that I was beginning to recognize when an episode was going to manifest itself so I could try to remove myself from the situation, before it started.

The back hall restroom was my only friend back then, I weathered many an episode there, but I'd get teased and bullied every time I came out of it. I could, to some extent, postpone an episode, but the longer I held out, the worse it would be when it hit. It was like an itch that you try to ignore, eventually it drives you crazy and you break and just have to scratch hard.

By my junior year, four sets of foster parents had grown tired of my condition and passed me on to the system again. But my fifth set of foster parents, Ben and Nancy Cohan, were nice. They didn't care about my Tourettes, they were the closest thing to real parents I had since mine had died in a car crash when I was eight. They encouraged me to pursue my art more aggressively as an outlet.

Nancy often asked if there were any boys I was interested in, or any friends I could hang out with. She was worried about my social life. That's about when I realized that here I was a teenaged girl, my body was developing and maturing even though I hid it under my hoodie, but I didn't seem to be attracted to anyone. At all. Period. Maybe it was the fact that people treated me so badly, that I was a freak. I just couldn't look at them in that way.

My senior year I spent a lot of time dwelling on this. I even snuck some peeks at porn from time to time to see if it would excite me, which it didn't, naked men were kind of gross. So I tried looking at some Playboy magazines, who knows, maybe I was a lesbian or something. But even though I didn't find the women's bodies gross I just wasn't interested in them either. Was I asexual? Did I even need a label?

Now not only was I still confused about my sexuality, but I had a poor body image when I compared myself to the women in the photos in those magazines.

I thought I was broken, so, much to my embarrassment, I experimented with masturbating. Just to find that it felt great, so physically I seemed to work fine. I just resigned myself to the probability that I'd never find a person who I was attracted to and would be alone my entire life. Is this how everyone feels? Is attraction just a story everyone tells themselves so they feel normal and not out of place?

I poured all my frustrations and my emotions into my art. My art teacher in my senior year, Miss Woods, always gave me special projects and submitted them to contests around the nation. I was winning art awards left and right as if I weren't already enough of a freak.

I turned eighteen that year and was removed from my foster parent's house because I was supposedly an adult now and aged out of the program, just adding to my frustrations in life. I stayed at a youth hostel for the remainder of my senior year.

The University of Washington awarded me a full ride scholarship, including room and board, for my art and academic record. I was ecstatic, college was going to be a life changer for me, no more bullies, no more mocking. I mean, everyone there was more mature right?

That illusion was actually destroyed my first week at UW, in one of the cafeterias I decided to study in while I ate lunch. I was hunched down in my hoodie, my utensils organized neatly and in the proper order on my napkin beside my chef salad as I skimmed my calculus book, absorbing the formulas.

I had just put my book down, aligned evenly with the table edge, so that I could get a bite of my salad when a familiar screechy voice rang out behind me.

"Well, if it isn't little miss spaz!"

I flinched as stress and anxiety hit me like a bulldozer. It felt almost like a physical blow. I turned to see Missy Hannigan, a cheerleader from my old high school, grinning like a hungry alligator. She was flanked by what I could only assume were her new little minions.

I could feel an "episode" coming on. I stood and tried to leave, but they blocked the way. My eyes were darting around looking for an escape, for a restroom. My shoulder started to twitch up to brush my cheek as I looked for a way around the girls. Missy just continued her verbal assault.

"They'll let any freak go to this university it seems. Why don't you just go to a community college and leave us normal people alone spaz?"

I blurted, "Physical derivative!" I was moving side to side trying to get around the girls as my shoulder twitched, brushing my cheek again. "Please let me go," I begged. The girls all laughed and I repeated, "The physical derivative."

Missy was suddenly pushed aside and a tall girl with a gorgeous mane of flowing brown hair stepped up to me, ignoring the shocked girls she had pushed through to my twitching self. She locked her intense, amber eyes that had an almost orange tint, on my green ones, as she grabbed my arm firmly.

"There you are!" Her eyes flickered to my book and back. "You are supposed to be tutoring me on my calculus."

She turned her gaze back to the other girls and I swear there was flame in her eyes. "Excuse us," she hissed as she pushed back through them, being sure to shoulder butt Missy on the way through.

Her hand moved from my arm down to my hand as she dragged me between tables, threading us smoothly to the restroom. "The derivative." I looked at the ground, trying to shrink away into nothingness as she opened the door and pushed me into the room. She looked under the stalls to make sure the room was empty and pushed me down onto a bench by the door.

The girl then turned around casually and put her back to the door effectively blocking it. Then she raised one foot against it to lean comfortably. I watched as she dug a pack of cigarettes out of her purse and lit one up. She looked up and took a deep drag, holding it in for a few seconds then exhaling. She finally looked down at me rocking on the bench, shrugging my shoulder to my cheek. "Derivative."

I didn't know what to say to her, and I didn't want to make eye contact I was so embarrassed by this whole incident. It wasn't supposed to happen like this in college, this isn't how it was supposed to be.

When the episode finally faded, I glanced up from the safety of my hood to see her watching me. It felt like she was studying me. Someone tried to push the door she was blocking closed, and the girl just turned her head slightly toward it and yelled, "Occupied!" I took the time to look her over.

She was stunning. I felt my stomach fluttering a bit as I took in her very feminine but slightly butch appearance. She was slim and tall, about 5'10" if I were to guess. Much taller than my 5'1". She had smallish breasts that still managed to fill out her faded black t-shirt in quite a pleasing manner. Her jeans hugged her legs, showing off the curves of her hips and calves. And for some bizarre reason the combat boots she wore were the perfect compliment to the outfit.

I looked up to her face. It held a contrast between an adorable girl next door look and something sexy and dangerous. She wore hardly any makeup, but her lips were full and looked awfully inviting. I was biting my lower lip. Then realized the thoughts I was having when I met her catlike eyes again. She was smirking. Shit!

I was immediately embarrassed about my thoughts and that she had caught me checking her out. I wasn't checking her out was I? I don't ever check people out. I was just curious about the girl that saved me from the bitch queen, right? I looked down at the floor and spoke, trying to divert the attention away from me, “Y-you shouldn't smoke. You're not a-allowed to smoke in public spaces. Th-th-those things will kill you.”

She snorted at me like I had just said the most absurd thing in the world, shaking her head she replied, “If only.” She put the cigarette out on the sole of her heel, dropping the butt on the tile floor, then held her hand out to me to take. “You done? Ready to go back out?”

I snapped at her a little too sharply, “I d-don't need your p-pity!” My mouth was tight with anger that shouldn't have been directed at her.

She looked more amused than taken aback by my aggression. “Not giving you any, just being friendly.” She kept her hand extended to me.

I slumped my shoulders in defeat and muttered hoarsely, “I'm sorry. Missy and the others are right, I'm a freak, I'd be better off dead.”

The next thing I knew, I saw white stars as a sharp pain and heat bloomed on my cheek where she had firmly slapped me, a tear was stinging the corner of my eye.

I looked up at her, slack-jawed and in shock, to see her gritting her teeth in anger. Her eyes were burning into me as she spoke through her clenched jaw, more calmly than her demeanor indicated. "Don't you EVER say that! Every day is a gift! It's how you fill that gift that defines you. Don't let senseless bitches like that Missy define you. Define yourself!"

I was stunned, unmoving. Her words echoing around in my head. Then she suddenly softened, her face changed to one of compassion as she raised her hand and placed it on my cheek, gently stroking with her thumb where she had struck. I caught myself wanting to lean into the warmth of her touch. "Sorry," I whispered as I suddenly stood.

She looked at me, then grabbed my hand and started dragging me back into the cafeteria. I liked the feel of her hand in mine, it gave me strength for some unknown reason. As we made our way back to my table, I saw her survey the room to make sure Missy was gone. Then she glanced back at me with a stunning smile.

"I'm Vee. Vee Taylor by the way."

I was much calmer now as I responded, "Ummm... hi. I'm Mia. Mia Jacobs."

We sat back at my table. I saw my plastic utensils were a little crooked and I went about straightening them up on the napkin and making sure it all aligned with the edge of the table. I noticed she was watching me do this intently. I tried to make small talk to divert her attention, I didn't want her to leave. “Vee? Is that short for something? Like Velma, Victoria, Valerie or some such?”

She nodded with a smirk and a mischievous smile lit her face while her eyes twinkled. “Yup, it stands for my name. Hey, you're not stuttering.”

I caught her misdirection so I answered with a smirk from inside my hood, “Yeah I only stutter when I'm nervous or stressed. Aaaaand, you didn't answer me, what is it short for?”

She cocked her head, like she was contemplating something, then said, “I thought it was cute, I got to hear more of your wonderful voice that way.”

She thinks my voice is wonderful? I started to smile then caught on again. “H-hey! Stop the misdirection woman, now spill!”

She laughed. It was pretty awesome, it was a real laugh that reached her sparkling eyes. I caught myself biting my lower lip again as she caved, rolling her eyes.

“Fine, I'll tell you, but virtually nobody knows. My dad was a Norse mythology professor, so he named me Valhalla, after the hall of the gods. It's been the bane of my existence.”

Wow. A unique name for such a unique girl. There was something different about her, and I found myself wanting to know more. I tried out her name. “Valhalla... Valhalla. Hmmm... I think I like that. It fits you. You...” I stopped and snapped my eyes to hers, tilting my head a bit.

She raised her eyebrows and asked, “What?”

I just smiled and shook my head and spoke a little wistfully, "Ummm... nothing. I just realized that this is already the longest conversation I have ever had with someone who isn't a teacher or a foster parent in like five years."

She smiled, but her eyes didn't share the smile, they looked a little... sad? Pained? She reached over with a hand and grabbed the top of my hood and stopped. "May I?"

I just nodded in trepidation and she pushed the hood off. My shelter, my personal hiding spot falling to my shoulders with it. Then she pushed my hair back over the hood and sat back to take me in.

Her eyes widened a bit. "Wow," she whispered almost inaudibly.

I don't think she meant to speak out loud. Then she smiled a genuine smile and locked eyes with me again.

"You really are stunning Mia, you shouldn't hide yourself away under that hood."

Is she flirting with me?

I could feel the heat of a blush on my cheeks and I found myself answering, "Ummm... I'll stop when you stop smoking." I grinned in triumph. Ha! Take that! I was about to raise my hood back up when she placed a warm, soft hand on mine to stop me.

"Deal!" she said with a triumphant grin of her own. She reached into her purse and pulled out her cigarettes and tossed them on the table.

She caught me glancing back and forth between her, the pack, and the table. I quickly reached out and turned the pack with an outstretched finger so the label was parallel to the edge of the table, nudging it till it was perfect, before retreating my hand back into my sleeve.

She took her lighter out of her purse and set it on the table next to the pack, looking at me sideways while making sure it was neatly lined up beside it. She tilted her head slightly, narrowing her eyes almost imperceptibly, observing me as she slowly pulled her hand back. When I did nothing, she smiled and sat back crossing her arms in satisfaction.

"So Mia, you know what this means right? We are going to have to hang out a lot together to make sure we hold up our ends of the bargain. You'll see me so much you'll get sick of me." She winked.

I said breathlessly, "Couldn't get sick of you." I slapped my hands over my mouth when I realized I said that out loud. I was wondering what the hell was wrong with me. I didn't understand since I had never felt anything like it before. Am I attracted to her?

She gave me a super-cute grin at that and put a hand out on the table, palm open, wiggling her fingers expectantly. "Cell me wench!" she said with mirth.

I looked at her eyes, then her hand, and I dug in my purse and handed her my cell phone timidly. She quickly entered her phone number, labeling herself 'She Who Shall Not Be Named' in the contact list. She handed it back and grabbed her cell out of her purse and passed it to me.

I looked at her with a smile. Technically she would be the first friend I have had since junior high. I entered my phone number and labeled myself 'Nicotine Patch' before absently handing it back to her. She glanced at it and snorted, then quickly overwrote it with 'THE Mia', showing me the screen, causing my cheeks to heat again.

She stood up and placed a hand on top of mine, still hiding in its sleeve. I could still feel the heat of her skin through the material.

"I gotta jet to class Mia. Russian Literature. Call me later, maybe we can hook up and do something one of these nights. I might text if I get bored." She started walking off, looking back at me.

I smiled at her bashfully. "O-okay. See ya, Valla." I swear I saw her stutter step and smile a bit wider when I called her Valla or did I imagine it?

I was about to stand and dump my tray with my uneaten meal in the trash and head off to class myself when my cell vibrated in my purse. I grabbed it and looked at the text message blazing away on it from "She Who Shall Not Be Named."

[bored already :)]

I quickly responded, [me 2 – tlk 2 u l8r]

I had a little skip in my step as I emptied my tray then gathered my things. I headed out to my art class with a smile on my face. It wasn't until later that day I realized my hood was still down. It didn't seem to bother me so much.

Chapter 2 – I'm so Confused

Art was more fun than in high school. We seemed to have more freedom to choose our own project and I really got into it. I decided to try taking little quarter inch squares of colored paper and arranging them to make a picture on my canvas. I could clearly see in my head which colors needed to go where to assemble the image I wanted to portray, and I calculated the quickest way to accomplish it by the end of class.

A minute before class ended I was finished. The instructor had been walking around checking everyone's progress. She approached me and looked at the seemingly random placement of the tightly packed squares on my canvas and asked if it was my take on impressionism. I realized why she asked and I just shook my head, then holding up my hand to indicate she should stay where she was, I walked across the room from her and held up my canvas.

The professor, Mrs. Sax, seemed genuinely shocked that she could clearly see what, to her, looked like a photograph of a tree swing in a meadow. I vividly remember playing there as a little girl, it was a happy time for me.

Mrs. Sax spoke, "Ummm... Miss Jacobs, tomorrow, I'd like to discuss this style with you a little bit."

As I made my way out the door to my next class I was a little confused but said, "O-okay Professor." Was it that bad?

After art class, the day seemed to crawl by slowly, but it was punctuated with my smiles as I received many random text messages from Valla throughout the day. I renamed her contact name to Valla on my phone, and we exchanged sarcastic barbs back and forth. Sarcasm is one of my superpowers.

I was in my final class of the day, Psychology when I got a text from Valla that I didn't know how to interpret or answer.

[out of class 4 day. Hitting frat party 2nite at 8. come with?]

I stared at the message for quite some time trying to read into it. I had never been to a party my entire life, not counting my birthday parties as a little kid. I don't really like being around people, they are only harsh around me. But I really wanted to be close to Valla.

"Come with?" Was that as a friend, or does it mean as a date? I can be her friend. I think I might be attracted to her. Was she flirting before? Is she gay? Am I gay? Does it matter? How do you act around a friend? I'm so confused. I straightened my back in resolve at the solution less likely to scare Valla off. Friends it is.

Finally, I answered back, [parties not my scene. Can't dance. Got nothing to wear n e way]. Almost immediately she responded, [tough wench. I b tempted to smoke so u gotta b there. U can use sum o my clothes. Meet my place 2nite at 7. we need 2 look hot :)]

I couldn't stop myself from smiling as I typed my response, [u r already hot. I'll hide behind u. if it sux I will bail tho :P]

[blush fine. Deal ;)]

Then we sent each other our dorm and room numbers. Suddenly I was both terrified and excited for class to get over with. I watched the second hand on the clock move at a painfully slow pace as I sharpened all of my pencils to the exact same length and listened to the endless droning lecture on the id, ego, and superego.

I grabbed a chicken salad sandwich on the way to my dorm and washed it down with a bottle of water. Then I entered my room, where I was the only occupant. Probably the only good thing that came from my Tourettes, I had an episode two days ago when I was moving in. My roommate, Gracie, freaked out and got the administration to give her a room change. Nobody else wanted to room with me, so yay, more space for the spaz!

As I studied, I started to get more and more nervous about the party. By the time seven o clock rolled around, I was sitting on the floor in the corner of my room with my hood pulled up over me. I was scared I'd induce an episode on my own. A few minutes later my cell phone rang. I grabbed it and saw it was Valla, I hovered over decline for a couple seconds but then couldn't resist talking to her and pressed accept. “H-h-hello?”

A cheerful Valla responded, “Hey chickadee, you're late! Get yer lazy ass over here, we got a party to get ready for!”

I smiled a little and tried to push the panic attack I seemed to be having away a little bit as I replied, “I ch-change-ed my mind. I can't g-go with you. I've never b-b-been to a party. People will be h-harsh to me.”

Her voice was cautious and tinged with concern. “You're stuttering again. I'm not making you nervous am I?”

I gave a quick laugh. “N-no, I actually feel braver around you. I just can't go to a party. Can I call you tomorrow?” I could hear the disappointment in her voice.

“Okay, see ya, Mia.”

I smiled a bit at the rhyme before I sighed as I hung up, “Bye Valla.” .

I just sat there in the corner a little while longer, slowing my breathing back to normal. Five minutes later there was a loud knock on my door.

I stood and walked over to it, cracking it open slightly and peeking through to see Valla standing there holding a bag up with a huge smile on her face. Her smile made my stomach flutter and my knees go a little weak. So that's what they mean when they say that. “What are you doing here?” I asked as she just pushed her way through to my room, throwing the bag on the first bed then turning to face me.

As she reached up and pulled my hood back down she squinted one eye and pointed, saying, “Hey! Off with that! We had a deal!” She reached both hands up and gathered my hair and pushed it out behind me, draping it over the hood. I trembled a bit when her hands brushed either side of my neck, her touch raising goosebumps on my skin. She seemed to notice this and smirked a little as she backed up a step to look at me.

"Much better," she sighed and grabbed my sleeve, pulling it up to reveal a hand. She grabbed my hand in hers and dragged me to the bed.

I was just smiling at her as I asked again, "What are you doing here Valla?"

She squinted and smiled, bobbing her head down in a cute manner when I called her Valla that I didn't fail to notice. "I like it when you call me that," she confirmed.

"Well, you said I make you braver. So here I am, bearing clothing for the party!" She grinned and grabbed the bag, opening it to reveal a few cute tops and some headbands. "You can't get out of this that easily, you don't even have to talk with anyone if you don't want. Remember, I promised we would leave if you didn't like it. I will be by your side the whole time. It's like any other party you've been to, just with more alcohol and cute guys... or uhhh... girls if that's what you're into."

She was looking at me a little sideways like she was fishing for something. I responded, "Well I wouldn't know what parties are like since the last one I was ever invited to we had a terrible pin the tail on the donkey incident that emotionally scarred us five-year-olds for life." I winked. Boy, I'm getting cocky!

"Once my Tourettes presented, I sorta became a social pariah, so no more invitations for Mia. As far as cute boys and girls go I really wouldn't know since I've never dated, and truthfully have really never EVER been attracted to anyone before. I must be busted. But

I guess it is hard to like the people that make your life a living hell, you know?"

I stopped myself from babbling and looked down at my feet, embarrassed I was sharing so much personal history with this person I had just met today. I think it just felt good to actually talk with someone. "Sorry, that's more than I have spoken in years. Sob story done. I'll shut up now."

She was just grinning at me. "No it's fine, I just feel privileged to be the person you unloaded on. I could listen to you read the phone book if I'm to be truthful. I love the alto resonance of your voice. Sooo... no dating? You ever been kissed?"

I shook my head, embarrassed but unable to break away from her dazzling eyes. She smiled and wiggled her eyebrows suggestively.

"Well, maybe we can find someone for you and change that tonight at the party. Here try this top on!" She offered a top.

I was resigned to the fact that she wasn't going to take no for an answer about the frat party, but somehow with her here it didn't seem so bad. "Let me shower first," I said as I walked into the bathroom shared between my dorm room and the one next to mine.

I locked the door to the other connecting dorm room, forgetting to lock my own, and pulled both my shirt and hoodie off in a single motion. I shimmied out of my pants, leaving me in my panties and bra. As I stepped toward the shower to turn it on, the door to my room swung opened and Valla walked in.

Her eyes went wide and the bag of clothes in her hand fell to the floor. I could feel her scan me from head to toe, her breath hitched and she looked at the floor quickly, biting her lower lip.

"Ummm... sorry, you got undressed really quick... I just thought you'd want to try a few of these on after your shower."

I tried covering my chest with my arms, wanting to shrink away into nothing. I really don't know why, I still had my bra on and she was a girl. It shouldn't matter, right? Why was she embarrassed too?

She looked back at the open door nervously then glanced back at my tight stomach and forced her eyes to mine.

"Umm... Okay, so I'll be out there." She started backing out of the room, pointing to the door with both hands and cocking her head toward the room.

Was she blushing? Pointing at the floor with both my hands I caught myself smiling. "Okay, and I'll be in here."

She finally made it out of the bathroom and shut the door. I could hear her muffled voice saying, "Yeah, Okay... Okay... I'll be out here."

I found myself smiling and blushing. I then had the most interesting shower of my life knowing Valla was out there. I felt so alive, almost... aroused?

After I dried off and used the blow dryer on my long ebony hair and on the mirror to defog it, I looked at myself. I guess I wasn't terrible looking. But I didn't look anything like the girls in those

Playboy's I looked at. Is that what attractive is? Then I'm seriously lacking. My c-cup breasts were nothing compared to the mammoth ones sported by those girls. Well at least I liked my full lips, they were my best feature I thought. Why did I suddenly care what I looked like?

I tried on every top she had brought over, I liked that they smelled like her, and finally settled on a white scoop-neck with a metallic gold swirl pattern on it. I grabbed a wide white hairband out of the bag and loosely pulled my hair back with it. Then I poked just my head out the door. "Hey, Valla. Can you grab me a clean pair of jeans and panties from my dresser, please? I forgot to bring some in. First and second drawer."

She smiled at me and stood from the bed and walked to the dresser and started digging through my clothes. "Ah-ha!" she exclaimed triumphantly as she walked over to the door, offering me my only pair of low-rise capri cut jeans, I must have been on drugs or something when I bought them.

I rolled my eyes at her and took them through the cracked open door along with the offered plain white cotton panties (I don't have any other kind), closing the door after me.

After pulling on the jeans, I looked in the mirror again. I virtually never wore makeup, but this was a party so I put on some eyeliner and a light brushing of purple eye shadow, barely enough to notice. Then I applied some pink lip gloss. Somewhat satisfied with the look I picked up my hoodie and pulled it over my head.

Grabbing the rest of the my clothes and Valla's bag I unlocked the connecting room door, then exited out my door to my room, dumping my dirty clothes into the laundry basket by the bathroom door. I saw Valla sitting on my bed, scanning my immaculate room with everything in its place, aligned perfectly.

Valla glanced over at me and stood up, frowning as she stepped up to me. “No, no, no, no, no Mia. I don't think so!”

Before I could stop her, she grabbed the bottom of my hoodie and pulled it up over my head as I squeaked in protest. Although to be completely honest I did raise my arms as she did it to make it easier for her to remove. I was staring at the floor embarrassed again.

I swiped my long hair back behind me with my hands, straightening the hairband and looked up at her. She was just staring at me, her mouth hanging open a bit.

“Crap!” I said, “That bad? I'll change into something else. Sorry.”

I started to turn as Valla blinked at me a couple times raising her hand. “Oh no! Don't you dare, you look smokin' hot Mia. Just throw some shoes on and let's get going, we're running a little late.”

I was blushing from head to toe. Did she just say I looked smokin' hot? I tried to hide the smile creeping up on my lips as I slid into some white sandals.

I finally took stock of Valla for the first time since she had arrived. She wore layered black and white tank tops that left a tempting amount of skin showing at her belly. Complimented by some black jeans and her signature combat boots. Somehow she made the outfit look completely feminine. I was entranced by the giant silver hoops hanging from her ears, drawing my eyes to her face.

I was barely able to grab my purse as she snagged my hand and dragged me out the door. It was already starting to feel comfortable, holding her hand like this. It seemed to be our natural state whenever we were moving. This thought made me blush a bit as we made our way out of the dorm and across the quad toward the frat houses. This was going to be interesting to say the least.

Chapter 3 – The Party

As we approached the frat houses in a comfortable silence, it was easy to tell which one was hosting the party. The music was booming and people were scattered all over the lawn in various degrees of intoxication in front of the giant Victorian house.

The smile never left Valla's face as she dragged me along and up the walkway to the covered porch, our fingers interlaced. She pushed the huge oak and glass paneled door open and passed into the incredibly loud music inside. I was surprised, there must have been over a hundred or so people crammed into the open living space. The central area had couples dancing to the beat while ringing around it were people standing around, drinking and chatting.

Valla skillfully threaded us through the crowd to the kitchen using her body to shield me the whole way. Once we arrived in the disorganized kitchen, it was little quieter and fewer people were milling around. I had to struggle with myself to keep from straightening up the glasses and fliers strewn about the counter haphazardly. Valla grabbed a couple red plastic cups from a stack and handed a fiver to the guy at the keg and he filled the two cups.

She tried to give one to me as she chugged her's half down, then shouted to me over the noise, "Here! Liquid courage! Let's take a second, and if you're ready let's get in there and do some dancing with some hotties!"

I took it from her with two fingers, like it would burst into flames, and took a whiff. That alone was enough to make me almost barf, like the big guy in the football jersey, was doing in the kitchen sink just then.

I took a tentative sip and had to fight back my gag reflex. I handed it back to her, shaking my head and shooting a scrunchy-nosed, disgusted look at it. “God, that smells and tastes like piss! Isn't underage drinking illegal?”

She smiled and winked, then downed the rest of her cup and then chugged mine down.

She dropped the cups into the overflowing trash can that I had a strong urge to clean up. She grabbed both of my hands and dragged us both back out to the main space and over to the stairs where we could look the party over.

Valla started swaying and bobbing her head to the beat as we stood there. I was just enjoying watching her when a large, muscular guy with a shaved head walked up to us. I slipped a little farther behind Valla. As he offered his hand to her, he yelled over the music, “Hey! I'm Rick!”

She took it. “Vee!” she yelled back shaking his hand, then stepping slightly to the side to reveal me a bit. “This is Mia!” He offered his hand and I shook it before he turned his attention back to Valla, and I hid behind her again.

“Wanna dance?” he shouted, offering his hand to her.

She smiled back, “Sure!” Valla grabbed his hand. She turned her head and winked back at me, ignoring my terrified look as she was dragged off to the dance area.

I could feel a pang of jealousy as I watched her gracefully gyrating and swaying with her arms above her head with that, that... Rick. God, she's breathtaking.

I was snapped back to the present when a blonde haired, stereotypical jock looking guy with a letterman's jacket stepped in front of me.

“Hey there! I'm Jake, wanna dance with me?” He offered a hand to me, expecting me to take it.

I crossed my arms over my chest and shrank back a bit. Not meeting his eyes. “I d-don't know how to.”

He didn't listen and grabbed one of my hands away from my chest with his own rough and calloused hand and dragged me toward the dance floor. “Nothing to it!” he shouted. He started dancing while I stood there. I glanced over at Vee, who hadn't seen me there yet, and I tried copying some of her motions.

The guy grabbed my hands in his rough ones and led me around, turning us fully six or seven times as we sorta danced. I wanted to go the other way to 'unwind' but he didn't. I was starting to panic trying to keep count of how may times we turned, and I was trying to pull away from him. But now his hands were all over my waist and back and wherever else he could touch. I pushed him away from me with both hands, starting to panic.

Just then someone stepped between us.

I looked up to meet Valla's eyes and much of that raising panic dissipated. She turned back to the guy, “She's with me. Beat it!”

The guy just raised his hands and backed off, turning to find another dance partner.

She turned to me smiling. “You okay Mia?”

I shook my head no and she grabbed my hand and dragged me upstairs to the restroom, pulling me inside and then closing the door and locking it.

In the relative quiet, the sound pressure had diminished, and I shifted back and forth on my feet. “You okay?” she asked softly.

I shook my head, I was too embarrassed to tell her.

“What is it?” she prompted. “Was it Mr. 'Put My Hands All Over You' out there?”

I took a breath and almost smiled at that and I could see that she caught it, giving a little smile herself.

I finally said really quickly, almost too quiet to hear, “That was creepy, but no. He got me twisted up and wouldn't let me unwind.” I looked anywhere but at Valla.

She put a finger on my chin and guided my gaze back to her eyes, I was mesmerized as I bit my lower lip. She prompted, “What do you mean? It's alright, you can tell me.”

I took a deep breath. “It's stupid really. I know it's irrational, but it's part of my obsessive compulsive disorder. I... feel like... there are invisible strings connected to me, and that when I turn around they twist around me like a cocoon. So I try to 'unwind' every time I turn around so that I don't get smothered by turning the same number of times the other way. I know they aren't really there, but dwelling on the visualization of them freaks me out so much I panic a little. I know as if I couldn't be any more of a freak, right?"

I crossed my arms over my chest to hide my hands in my armpits. I missed the seclusion of my hoodie right now, and I was fighting myself not to start unwinding in front of her.

"You still need to 'unwind'?" she asked, lowering her head to keep eye contact.

I fought back a tear and nodded my head.

She smiled. "Okay, don't mind me. When you're done, I was kinda hoping you'd dance... with... me?" She looked down bashfully.

I took a ragged breath and started to slowly turn counter clockwise, stopping to look at her after the first turn. She didn't look appalled. Instead, she was biting her lower lip with her head tilted. That made butterflies appear in my stomach as I kept turning. Once I counted eight turns, it felt right again, I didn't feel the invisible constriction.

So I lowered my head. "Ummm... some party huh?"

She raised her eyebrows, shooting me an almost seductive smile that made me warm in some inappropriate places. "It's about to be." She grabbed my hand, lacing our fingers as she opened the door and dragged me out and back downstairs.

I'd follow her anywhere like this.

Without hesitation, she grabbed my other hand and backed into the dance floor, dragging me along, keeping eye contact the whole way, a grin on her face. She used her body as a shield, pushing through the other dancers till we were in the middle of the room.

She released my hands and with a big knee buckling smile, she raised her hands above her head and started bouncing with the beat. I looked at her from bottom to top, and unconsciously licked my lips and raised my arms into the air and copied her actions.

This wasn't too bad, I was starting to have fun and let loose when the song ended. Since it was getting later in the night, a slow song kicked in and I begun to turn to leave the dance floor when Valla snaked a hand in to grab mine and turned me back toward her.

She pulled me close and grabbed my arms and put them on her hips and she draped hers over my shoulders. She leaned down and placed her mouth next to my ear.

"This is nice, I like dancing with you."

Her hot breath on my neck caused goosebumps to shoot down my skin. I just nodded and continued swaying with her.

She led us around in lazy circles. I wasn't paying any attention to how many times we were turning, I was so lost in the warmth of her body and the slight vanilla scent coming from her that my imaginary strings didn't seem to matter. I was vaguely aware that she changed the direction of our circles from time to time. Is she counting for me?

We spent almost an hour out there, through various songs. Dancing and joking and laughing. We seemed to always keep contact with each other at all times. I don't remember the last time I had so much fun.

We noticed the party was slowly winding down and she grabbed my hand without a word. Interlacing our fingers as she dragged me through the dwindling crowd toward the door, only to stop short when a girl blocked our path.

Shit! It was Missy, sneering at us.

“Now I understand why you're helping the spaz! You're that Vee girl that got kicked out of so many high schools for fighting for the damn freaks like her. We don't need your kind here, so why don't you just take your pet spaz there and leave?”

Valla dropped my hand and I saw it clench into a fist as she quickly raised it to take a swing at Queen Bitch. She had been kicked out of other schools for fighting? For protecting others? I knew Missy was just baiting her and I quickly placed a hand gently on Valla's fist. Almost too quietly to be heard over the music I said, “Don't.” I could feel the tenseness flow away from her fist as she unclenched it, and she looked at me locking our eyes. Her shoulders visibly relaxed.

Missy snorted, “Ha! Takes a freak to tame the infamous Vee huh? What? Are you dykes too?” Vee's fist reappeared and I stepped between the girls, shooting Valla a pleading look.

She relaxed again, grabbing my hand and dragging me away shouting, “She's not worth it!” Shoulder checking Missy again as we passed.

She pulled me through to the kitchen again, and out the backdoor to a huge deck and sat us down on a bench near the door.

Her demeanor changed instantly. She was all grins and excitement when she looked at me. “So? How was your first party?”

I smiled, then idly picked up a random red plastic cup noticing the inside was white. I set it back down and looked beside the door where dozens of stacks of plastic bags full of unused cups were sitting, marked '250 count'. They must have been stocking up for the new school year.

I smiled warmly back at her as I spoke, “The first part was terrifying, I thought for sure it was going to trigger an episode. But my other neurosis kicked in with that Jake guy, which embarrassed me anyway. The rest of the party was heavenly. I had so much fun dancing and laughing with you.” I blushed at the last admission. “Though the last part with Queen Bitch... not much fun.”

She grinned back nervously. “So... ummm... did you think Jake was cute?”

I snorted back, rolling my eyes. “Not so much. He was hairy and his hands were rough, and he was so grabby. I tried to like him, but he just didn't seem attractive to me.”

She brightened up, her eyes sparkled a bit. “Was there anyone else that you may have liked in there?”

I suddenly got coy and stood up, lazily walking a couple steps to the door and absently grabbed a few bags of red cups from the stacks. I looked back at her as I started opening the bags. “Well, ummm... I th-think for the first time in my life, I-I actually f-found myself attracted t-to someone.”

“Anyone I'd know?” she asked.

I didn't answer instead I walked to the far side of the deck, well aware of her intense gaze on me as I sat down and started placing cups down in rows across the entire deck, some right side up and some upside down, often skipping a placement. I glanced back at her with a shy grin. “So, can you tell my why you seem to be saving me all the time? Missy implied you do this sort of thing often. Did you really get kicked out of schools for fighting?”

I started placing cups faster and faster as she spoke.

“Well, yeah, I don't like people who pick on anyone who is different. I think everyone is beautiful in their own way and we should celebrate these differences, not persecute people for them.”

I was now putting cups down in rows as fast as I could.

“So it tends to get me into a little trouble,” she finished.

I looked back at her for a second as I was starting to run out of cups just to see her walking toward me with a few more bags of them. She just opened the bags and set them beside me before returning to the bench. I cocked my head at her then turned back to my cups and kept placing them as I spoke, “You seemed awfully mad. Are you sure that's the only reason?”

There was silence for a few seconds, the only noise was the placement of cups. Did I overstep? I was getting nervous, but then she spoke quietly.

“It's mostly because I understand. I've spent most of my life in and out of hospitals. People tend to treat you different like you are either fragile, broken, or a freak. I'm no different than anyone else. My condition is not who I am. So I can't stand watching anyone go through... that... I don't know.”

Over half of the deck was filled with rows of cups now and more cups kept magically appearing next to me whenever I ran low. She moves quietly. I asked over my shoulder, “What's wrong with you? If you don't mind me asking.” I heard her take a deep breath as my hands were flashing, placing cups at a breakneck speed.

She whispered, “I'd rather not discuss it. I'm fine right now, that's all that matters.”

She delivered the last bag to me and returned to her seat. She tried to change the topic. “So whatcha doin' there Mia?” she asked in a chipper voice just as I placed the last cup.

I glanced back to see her raise her eyebrow as she realized that the last cup finished my last row perfectly.

I smiled at her and just opened my palms toward my creation. “You asked me earlier, if I found someone here attractive.” I nodded at the cups. She looked at me sideways with confusion in her eyes. Then I realized why. I looked at her sheepishly, remembering that not everyone has a broken brain, "Oh... sorry, follow me."

It was my turn to grab her hand and drag her back into the house, my breath hitched as she laced our fingers and started rubbing the back of my hand with her thumb as we went. I almost tripped as I got a little weak in my knees because of it. I dragged her up the stairs and into a room with a rear facing window. I smiled at her and opened the window wide and motioned down, stepping aside.

I was embarrassed about my admission below so I looked at my feet, suddenly seemingly fascinated with my sandals. I heard her breath catch as she leaned out the window.

"Holy shit!" she exclaimed. "That is fucking amazing Mia... YOU are fucking amazing!"

I glanced up at her and she was just leaning out the window, her hands gripping the window frame, staring down onto the deck with a huge smile. I stepped to her side, catching a hint of her vanilla fragrance and glanced down at my handiwork as she absentmindedly grabbed my hand while we looked down.

Sure, the arrangement in red and black where I omitted cups looked like a rough, pixelated photo of Valla, drawn in the sea of white cup insides. But the red 'Valla' I spelled at the bottom might have given it away. I was muttering,"If there were more cups I could have made it more realistic. I'm still not satisfied with it. I could have done better. If I would have taken a few more seconds to determine the..." My obsessive rambling was interrupted by her lips meeting mine.

People always talk about how they wish their first kiss could be magical like you see in the movies. But from what I understand the reality of it all is that it rarely is. I never thought I'd ever get a first kiss, let alone enjoy it since I had determined I was pretty much asexual. But wow! Just wow!

Every part of my body was buzzing with heat, my mind was blank. It's never blank, always going over things, analyzing things, obsessing over things. Her soft lips pressing against mine, and our lip gloss slowly sliding together was so sensual it was mind blowing.

I was barely able to mentally kick myself for just standing there and got myself to return the kiss, leaning into it. I felt her tongue gently outlining my lower lip, asking for permission to enter. I opened my mouth slightly, deepening the kiss as I raised my hands to cup her face. I tentatively allowed my tongue to touch hers, and then I couldn't get enough as hers gently swirled around mine. Taking control of me. Owning me. I eagerly surrendered to her.

Regrettably she broke our kiss a few seconds later, our lips sticking slightly from our mixed gloss, both of us gasping for air. This is the first time in my life I was frustrated that oxygen was needed to sustain life. I missed her lips already, I realized I was curling my toes. I could feel the burn of a blush spreading on my cheeks and down my neck. I knew that I needed to form some sort of coherent thought, but none came.

She smiled so softly at me, with a new hungry look sparkling in her orange eyes. “Ummm... I didn't think I was gay before that kiss. Boy was I wrong!” She giggled at her admission with a genuine smile, staring at my lips and licking her own.

Somehow I found myself saying with a tinge of wonder in my voice, “I'm pretty sure I'm Valla-sexual now myself.”

We both laughed with our eyes locked on each others.

She glanced nervously between me and the cup art below. She pecked my lips quickly and said, “Just a sec Mia.” She grabbed her cell out of her purse and took a photo of the cup art. She then turned back to me biting her lower lip, a look of want on her face. “Uhhh, I think we need to talk.”

I nodded shyly.

She continued quickly, “My dorm is closer, my roommate should be out all night.” Then she grabbed my hand, lacing our fingers and dragging me out of the room as we headed for the quad.

Chapter 4 – Poetry

We arrived at her dorm room with her dragging me inside, closing the door and leaning with her back against it. I don't know how long it took us to get there, I was still obsessing over the way her lips felt on mine.

She smiled at me, tilting her head slightly as she studied me. "When's your first class tomorrow? I only have American Literature at 3:00," she stated.

I thought for a second. "I only have two classes in the afternoon tomorrow. My Tuesday, Thursday schedule. Art and calculus. Art is at 1:00."

She nodded. "I know we have to talk. What happened tonight was HUGE... and scary, and exciting! At least to me. But I really am exhausted, you mind if we just sleep and talk in the morning?"

I didn't know what to say. "Ummm... sure. It was huge for me too. Like, life altering huge. But just standing here I can feel my own exhaustion creeping in."

She smiled warmly in understanding and wandered over to a dresser, and grabbed out two sets of boxer shorts and two oversized t-shirts and tossed me a set. She winked and said, "Mine's the bed in the corner there, be right back." Then she disappeared into her bathroom.

I undressed and got into the sleeping clothes she gave me. I could smell her vanilla scent on the shirt, it gave me a warm tingly feeling. I sat on the edge of her bed to wait and looked down at the open notebook sitting next to the pillow. I read the words on the page, it was a poem. The disjointed cadence of it and the lack of consistent rhyme gave more ambiance to the emotional words on the paper. I could empathize and feel the emotion on the page.

"Wow," I whispered and started thumbing through the pages. Each one was more amazing than the last. I felt eyes on me and glanced up to see Valla looking intently between me and the notebook. I handed it quickly to her, averting my eyes. "Sorry," I whispered.

She took it and held it to her, hugging it to her chest. "It's okay. They really aren't good enough for anyone else to read."

I shook my head. "My God Valhalla, those poems were amazing. I could read those all day."

She blushed and set it on the nightstand. I saw her shiver and bite her lower lip at the use of her full name. Then wordlessly she opened the covers, motioning down to the bed with her eyes. I silently obeyed and slid into bed under the covers, my back to her and she slid in behind me, pressing the front of her body against my back and wrapping her arm over my waist possessively.

I stopped breathing. I sat there stock still, terrified of moving or saying anything that could ruin this intimate feeling. The last sleepover I had was when I was six, and it didn't feel anything like this. I could feel the warmth of her body where it touched me. We were a perfect fit as she molded around me. I smiled thinking, I'm the little spoon.

She put her lips on my neck and breathed hotly. "Mia?"

I squeaked out an almost silent, "Yeah?"

She kissed my neck, causing a shiver to spread down my body. "Breathe," she ordered.

"Oh," I said as I finally exhaled the breath I had been holding.

She giggled a little. "Goodnight Mia."

I sighed and relaxed back into her, feeling even more contact. "G'night Valla." I couldn't have taken more than five or so breaths before I was taken by the most relaxing sleep I had ever experienced.

I woke up to the sun shining in through the window and the bed shaking with an over-enthusiastic, bubbly soprano voice squealing at Valla and I. It was speaking at speeds faster than a chipmunk on speed.

"Oh, my Gawd! You two are so cute! Are you like a couple? If not you should be. You should see how cute you are. Here!" She snapped a picture with the phone in her hand then showing her screen to us.

"Oh wait. Like you could totally be my hawt lipstick lesbian roommate Vee! I could like, hook up with all the cute guys that show up trying to catch you two together! How cool would that be? So pleeeeeease say you are a couple! Wait, if I think yer hawt, does that mean I'm a lesbian? Ooooo I'd so make an awesome lesbian!

Maybe I should try to hook up with a girl at my next party! Oh! We could like double date and stuff!"

We both sat up stunned. What the hell is going on? Who is this? Valla tightened her grip on my waist protectively, turning us almost imperceptibly so she was between the crazy little peppy blonde explosion on the bed, and myself. My eyes were darting everywhere looking for an escape.

"Vicky!" Valla shouted over the blonde pixie. "Vicky, calm down! Slow down, you are talking on fast forward again!"

The blonde girl stopped bouncing, smiled back and forth between us and finally stopped talking, looking at Valla eagerly.

Valla saw my discomfort and moved her arm from my waist and moved it up to my shoulders, hugging me in and allowing me to bury my face in her shoulder to hide. "You calm now Vickster?" she asked. The tiny blonde just nodded quickly, her smile not fading.

I felt Valla squeeze my shoulder reassuringly before she spoke, "Vicky, this is Mia, she's my... well I'm not sure how we define ourselves yet since we haven't had time to talk."

Vicky shot her hand forward toward me. "Pleased to meet you Mia!" she said quickly and enthusiastically.

I timidly reached out the hand that wasn't holding onto Valla's shirt for dear life. "I'm p-p-pleased to m-meet you too Vicky."

Before she let go of my hand, she squeaked, "Oh my Gawd! Just how cute are you!?" She sat back on the end of the bed and looked at Valla.

God help me, but a picture of a hyperactive puppy waiting expectantly for its owner to throw a ball shot through my mind.

"So are you? Huh? You know... a lesbian Vee?" She asked with wide eyes.

Valla hugged me, kissing the top of my head before she spoke, "Well, to my own surprise, it appears so. Since all I dreamed about the entire night was kissing Mia again."

I stiffened for a second at her admission then snuggled in tighter since that's all I had been thinking about too until this wild blonde woman woke us the heck up.

"I have the coolest roommate EVER!" Vicky bubbled and swung her head dramatically to turn her enthusiasm toward me. "So how did you meet? Was it like, love at first sight? Is she like, a good kisser? I bet she is!"

I couldn't stop myself from laughing a little as I replied, "Sh-she slapped m-me. I'll let y-you know. And, hell yes! But I d-don't have much to base th-that on as it was my first kiss ever." Where did that burst of confidence come from?

I smiled up at Valla, who stuck her tongue out at me.

Vicky crossed her arms over her heart and hugged herself as she rocked back and fourth before looking up. "Gawd! That is soooo cool and sweet! Your very first kiss! And it was a lesbian kiss!

How frickin' hawt is that? I'm jealous! Wait, ooooo, I can get a new first kiss too if I start mackin' on a girl at my next party! I bet I'm gonna love it!"

I was blushing hard now. Valla glanced at her alarm clock and grabbed a pillow with her free hand and threw it at Vicky. "Hey, don't you have a class in like a half hour? Leave my Mia alone and give us some privacy you hyperactive debutante!"

My Mia? Swoon!

Vicky faked a pout then smiled, hopping up into our personal space. "Okay! One for you," she kissed Valla on the cheek and leaned down to me. "And one for you!" She kissed my cheek then bounded over to her side of the dorm room and grabbed her purse. "Bye ladies!" She waved a tiny wave at us before she bounded out the door.

I caught myself giving a tiny wave back as I looked at Valla in shock. "What the hell was that!?" She snorted, I thought it was cute.

"That..." She leaned down and captured my lips in a soft kiss. "Was..." She kissed me again, brain function was diminishing. "My..." A third, lingering kiss. "Roommate."

I moaned happily and blinked rapidly, clearing my head as she continued speaking.

"I'm so sorry about her, I think her parents were a chipmunk and a cheerleader. But she means well. I didn't even think about her seeing us. Please don't be mad we were outed that way when we don't even know what 'we' are. God, if word gets out... not everyone will be as understanding. This will make life harder if you decide you want this... if you want me. I'm sorry Mia."

I snuggled into the crook of her neck, thinking while absently kissing at her pulse point. I felt her shiver before I spoke. "I'm whatever you want me to be. I couldn't give a flying fuck in space if people give me flack for wanting you. If that makes me gay, fine. They couldn't treat me any worse than they do now. Because I do... I want you. I've never wanted anyone in my life, this is so strange to me. You told me that every day is a gift. That we define ourselves by how we fill it. Well, I want to fill my days with you, to define myself that way. If you aren't comfortable with it, I can be your secret or just your friend. But I don't want to have you NOT in my life."

She looked at me. Her sparkling eyes were watery, on the verge of tears. "I want you too," she whispered as a single tear rolled down her cheek.

I have known her for a day and still I never thought I would ever see this woman cry.

I reached up and brushed the tear away with my thumb.

She continued, "So where do we go from here? Does that make us girlfriends, or do we date first? I don't want to move too fast for you. Life is too short, I'm all about living in the now, but I can wait for you to be ready."

I took a deep cleansing breath. "I-I can be your girlfriend," I whispered into her smiling kiss.

To alleviate the heavy tone that hung thick in the air, I looked at the door with a chuckle. “I didn't think airheaded blondes really existed!”

Valla giggled, shaking her head. “Don't be fooled. She may be super sweet and hopped up on sugar, but she's like soooo beyond genius. She has an eidetic memory and an IQ off the charts. 4.0 student because of it. She's a business major here.”

I stared at her unbelievably and shook my head. “Who woulda thought?”

We spent the next few hours talking about everything, learning as much as we possibly could about each others lives and defining what we were to each other. That was more intimate to me than all our kissing combined, I could feel our attachment growing.

We covered everything, from our childhoods to the cup art I made for her last night. She forwarded the photo of it to my phone so I could make it my avatar for her in my contact list. I really liked her middle name, Abbey. It suited her much better than mine, Jessica. The only topic she wouldn't discuss was the reason for her visits to the hospital.

It was getting close to noon, so after getting dressed she walked me back to my dorm room so I could get ready for the day. She looked around at the uber-organized room and spoke to me through the bathroom door as I was drying off from my shower, “You don't have a roommate?”

I laughed. “Nope. Nobody want's to room with 'the spaz', I might 'infect' them or something.”

She laughed a bit. “Sooooo, hyper-blonde free privacy?”

I could almost see her suggestive look and wiggling eyebrows through the door. I snorted at the image. “Yeah, privacy you perv.”

She laughed back. “Cool. I know where I'll be hanging out a lot now.”

I finished getting dressed and walked out into the room brushing my long hair. Valla was sitting on my bed with a pen, writing on one of my notepads. She put them down on the nightstand when I came out to sit down beside her, still brushing. “Allow me,” she said, taking the brush and running it through my silky hair.

I closed my eyes and just basked in the intimate attention for a minute.

I opened my eyes for a second, glancing over at the nightstand and seeing the crooked notepad with the pen sitting on it. I tried to ignore it, shutting my eyes again to enjoy the attention. But then I opened one eye leaned over and nudged the notepad until the bottom aligned with the edge of the stand, then did the same with the pen before sitting back up and closing both eyes as she kept brushing.

I could hear Valla breathing a little heavy. “Is it wrong for me to think that it's, to borrow a phrase from Vicky, friggin' hawt, when you do that?”

I snorted. “You'd be the only one.” My hair was brushed to one side and I gasped when I felt her soft lips at my pulse point, gently kissing and sucking.

I was starting to breath raggedly when she pulled back.

“Okay lady, let's get some lunch before your class, we didn't eat any breakfast so you need to fuel up.”

I was still breathing heavily, trying to get the heat between my thighs to dissipate. “You friggin' tease!” I whispered, but couldn't help but smile at her evil giggle.

With that, we were off to forage for lunch before I had to head off to my art class. I couldn't believe it when she grabbed my hand and laced our fingers, walking so close our legs brushed together. She was unafraid to show her feelings for me in public. I felt so lucky and proud to have her by my side.

We chatted while we ate. I found every facet of this woman fascinating. We overheard some passing students talking about the awesome urban artwork someone found after last night's party. Valla and I shared an 'Oh my God!' look with each other and laughed.

I was starting to get anxious as I noticed that a lot of the guys that walked by would notice me. A few looked at me like I was a piece of meat, I wasn't used to people being able to see me. I missed my hoodie, but I felt safer with Valla by my side. She seemed to read my mind.

“See? I told you were beautiful. You shouldn't hide yourself away. You are gorgeous and should show it with pride to the world. Those guys can look all they want and be jealous 'cause they can't have you. I already claimed you for Vee-opolis!”

My cheeks burned in a moment of confidence I said with a flirty tone, “Does that mean I get the key to the city?” I wiggled my eyebrows suggestively.

She giggled and blushed slightly and replied without missing a beat, “Freely given.”

Then all too soon we finished our lunch and it was off to class. I whispered to her as we emptied our trays into the trash can, “You make me brave.” I implied our previous conversation about the hoodie. She shot a dazzling toothy smile at me, her eyes sparkling and saying more than any words could convey.

She shocked me further when she kissed me openly outside of my classroom, promising to be back to walk me to calculus later. Some people were smiling when I walked to my desk, but one of the girls in the room shot me a disgusted sneer. I heard someone fake cough “Dyke!” behind me. Real mature. It amazed me how polarizing sexuality could be for the people sticking their noses in your personal life. Why is it anyone else's business who I'm attracted to?

I simply ignored them as I settled in at my workstation. A text buzzed on my phone, I looked at it.

[miss u already]

Blushing I quickly texted back, [miss u more], just as the instructor walked in.

Chapter 5 – Art

Mrs. Sax started walking over to me soon after class began, stopping at various other students to answer questions as she approached. I was looking at a bunch of large bottles filled with plastic beads of different colors. I popped them open and poured them out across my work surface with a smile. I grabbed a new canvas, laying it flat beside the beads and picked up a glue bottle.

I started gluing beads to the canvas in rows as Mrs. Sax arrived at my workspace and addressed me. “So, Miss Jacobs...”

I turned my attention to her as she spoke, absently grabbing beads and gluing them onto the canvas without really looking.

“I showed the piece you created yesterday to the other art professors. You did that in an hour and a half.” It was a statement, not a question.

I couldn't read her expression. I steeled myself for the 'You can apply yourself better' lecture. I looked down shyly, understanding her disappointment while my hands continued gluing beads. “S-sorry, I could have d-done better, but I had to scale back to make sure it was done by the end of class. I'll d-do better with this one, I'll just work faster.” Concern creased my face. I liked art, I didn't want to upset the instructor.

She placed a hand on my shoulder. “No hun, I didn't mean it like that, I meant that it was simply amazing you could accomplish that in such a short period of time. You know you don't have to do a project in a single class... you can take as long as you need."

I relaxed a bit and exhaled.

I glanced back up at her shaking my head a little. "I kinda have to, it's just the way it works with me... sorry ma'am. I'd drive myself up a wall if I left it unfinished overnight, I'd lose too much sleep." She tilted her head and regarded me, I'm pretty sure she was trying to figure out my damage.

She continued with curiosity in her voice, "You didn't once move away from your canvas yesterday, how were you able to see what you were doing well enough to know what it looked like at a distance?"

I just shrugged at her as my hands kept working. "I can just see it in my head. I just take whatever material I have and make my collages. Sometimes it is hard since I convince myself I have to use every piece, so I have to get creative and devise a grid in my head before I start to utilize it all. It's just like math, I can just sorta see the answer."

She looked shocked. "You do it in your head?"

I shrugged again. "Well, yeah. Isn't that how artists work? Visualize your painting or drawing or sculpture in your head and create what you envision?"

She chuckled holding her hands up in surrender. "Touche. But you are on a whole other level. Do you have other pieces? And would you be interested in submitting your work into national competitions or selling your work at the art auction at the end of the quarter? I'm sure there will be great interest."

I stopped working for a second, blushing at her compliments as I reached for my phone in my purse with my free hand. I pulled up the photo of my cup art from last night and handed the phone to her as I started working again. "I made that with some plastic cups for my... ummm... my 'girlfriend' last night at a party. I don't have any more I gave all my work from high school to my art teacher at the end of the year since I lived in a youth hostel and didn't have any place to store them." My heart soared while referring to Valla as my girlfriend. That just brought up the memory of her lips on mine and my heart skipped a beat. Mmmm.

"You did this with plastic cups? How long did it take you?" She asked.

Ahh, I know what she's getting at! I nodded. "Yeah, I could have done better, but I was limited by a number of available cups. That's why it's so rough. It took around 10 minutes and 13 seconds to make."

She shook her head with an odd smile on her face. "Hon, you gotta stop putting down your work. I've never seen anything like this skill you have. It is a true gift."

I chuckled at her statement. "You'd be the first to think my obsessive compulsions are a gift."

She kept looking between my working hands and my eyes as we spoke. She went on to discuss not only entering my work in art competitions but possibly at student gallery showings as well. I still didn't think it was good enough, but she convinced me to agree.

I was counting down in my head, it was close to the end of class. I looked up at the clock to verify. Yup, two minutes till class was out and I reached for the last bead and came up with nothing. I started to panic and turned away from her and started scanning the work surface, then looking at the ground mumbling under my breath, “Where is it? It has to be here... I can't finish. I know it was here...”

Mrs. Sax must have realized what I was doing when she uttered shyly, “Oh.”

I looked at her to see her rolling the last bead between her fingers.

“Sorry Miss Jacobs. Here.” She offered the bead and I grabbed it and glued it in place at the end of the final row.

I relaxed, thirty seconds left. “Done!” I exclaimed. I looked at her and cocked my head, tilting it down a bit to indicate she should stay. She smiled at me with an excited glint in her eyes as I walked across the room with the beaded canvas.

I turned it up for her to see the seascape, with the pier by the ferries that I used to walk along whenever I needed to think and get away from everything. I was almost happy with this one, a few more beads and it could have been better.

“Amazing!” she said cupping her hands to her face almost like a prayer.

As I walked back and placed the canvas by my other materials and made sure it was parallel to the tabletop.

“See you tomorrow Professor Sax,” I said as I retrieved my purse and book to head to calculus. “Please, call me Jenny,” she said. Then added while handing me her business card, “Would you mind sending me that photo of your cup art?”

I smiled at her. “No problem. And please, call me Mia. My mother was Mrs. Jacobs.” Before I left, I caught the look of pity on her face at my use of 'was'.

I took a single step out the door and was met by a grinning Valla. She gave me a quick peck on the lips and grabbed my hand as we started walking.

“I sooo missed you while you were in there. You're like a drug to me. A drug that kisses reeeealy good!” She smiled with the excitement of a little kid in a candy store... I blushed.

“I missed you too Valla.” I giggled and laced our fingers, giving her hand a squeeze as we made our way to my calculus class. I sighed, I never wanted to let her go. But the moment was ruined by that same fake cough, “Dykes!” coming from behind us.

I had to grasp her hand tighter to prevent her from turning to confront the ass-hat.

“Just ignore people like that. I've lived with harassing crap like that for a long time, gay slurs are just new kindling for their fire. They are just ignorant, or jealous, or both. I mean, you are quite a catch.”

I grinned ear to ear at her, winking. She relaxed and returned the smile.

I suddenly perked up. "Oh! By the way! I was super psyched when I got to call you my girlfriend to my art instructor! She liked the cup you." I'm sure my eyes were twinkling as she leaned down for a quick kiss. The way she towers over me is just so damn sexy!

She murmured into my lips, "Why does that make me hot? You sure you have to go to class?"

I blushed and admitted, "I'd probably go nuts obsessing over it if I skipped out."

She nodded in understanding as we arrived at my class. She leaned down and gave me a soft, barely there kiss on my lips and slipped a folded piece of paper into my hand, shooing me inside.

I giddily staggered into my class with a goofy grin on my face, I turned back to Valla's voice calling after me, "I gotta get to American Literature. Wait for me here after class and I'll walk you back to the dorms."

I nodded to her with a content sigh, watching her scoot off.

I sat in a back chair, setting my book down on the desk, carefully aligning it to the desk edge. I still had a minute before the lecture began, so I unfolded the paper Valla had handed me. My breath caught, it was a poem. A poem in her wonderfully looping handwriting. Titled "Every Day".

The words seemed to have a life of their own, they spoke to me in an intimate manner. I read it over and over and over. Absorbing it. It was as if it were speaking my inner thoughts about her.

I was so lost in it a smile crept across my face. I poured over it for a few minutes, then I was aware of my name being called by the professor.

"Miss Jacobs, since you seem too preoccupied to pay attention to the lesson you must already know the answer to the formula on the board. Care to come up and work out the answer, if it isn't too much trouble for you that is?"

I tried to shrink away. Why didn't Valla let me wear my hoodie? I glanced nervously at the formula quickly and saw the answer in my head, then spoke meekly, "I-I d-don't need to work it out. I-it is one s-sixth the cosign of 2 X cubed."

The professor looked at the board then at me, squinting his eyes with a frustrated, accusatory look on his face for a painfully long second. I averted my eyes to the floor. He didn't address me again but just continued his lecture as some of the other students mumbled.

I just wanted to disappear, until I remembered Valla's poem. My smile returned as my eyes shot to it and I drank it in again, memorizing every line, every letter, and every emotion.

I was relieved when class got out and I stood by the door, watching people pass by noticing a couple guys check me out. After five minutes, the looks were really getting to me. I started looking around self-consciously for a place to hide when a warm arm snaked around my waist from behind, fingers tracing circles on my side, the scent of vanilla and something uniquely Valla clouding my head.

“Hey,” Valla whispered in my ear, her hot breath on my ear caused a delightful shiver to run through me.

I turned with a grin. “Hey.” It was amazing, any apprehension and anxiety I had moments before just melted away just looking into her mesmerizing eyes. I bit my lower lip bashfully as she moved her arm from my waist and grabbed my hand as we started walking.

She stopped suddenly. “Oh! I have something for you!” She rummaged around in her purse and pulled out an adorable three-inch tall white teddy bear with a pink bow who was holding a little heart.

She held it out to me biting her smiling lower lip and swinging from side to side in an adorable manner. “Here. You said you feel braver when I'm around. This is 'Little Vee', she can protect you when I'm not around!”

I accepted her with a huge smile and hugged Valla, basking in the warmth of our contact. Feeling her breasts pressed against my upper chest, it felt, I don't know – right?

“Little Vee huh? She's adorable!” I whispered as she released me from the hug. I took another look at the teddy before carefully putting her into my pocket. Before I could look back up, I was being pulled down the hall towards her dorm.

Chapter 6 – Halloween Party

The weeks seemed to fly by, each day Valla and I getting closer and closer. I had to admit, I was addicted to her. I couldn't imagine myself without her strength, compassion, insight and emotional empathy beside me. I had segmented my life into two distinct sections, 'before Valla' and 'with Valla', and determined that I was so much better off 'with Valla,' not to mention exponentially happier.

We had learned almost every facet of each other, every secret, every need, every dream. Everything except her health which nagged at me endlessly. I had to put it in the cubbyhole of my mind reserved for things I would eternally obsess over but realized they were always there but could never do anything about just so I didn't go crazy. She would tell me when she was ready.

I especially treasured the times Valla would take me on 'official' dates. She treated me like a princess. I couldn't have been more hers if I had tried. She enjoyed the rare times I would get brave and take charge some nights. I even got the nerve to set up one of our dates once.

Our physical relationship had progressed a little slower. I could tell that she didn't want to rush me and I didn't want to scare her with the fact that I would have given myself to her without a thought, at a moment's notice if she wanted me. As it was things hadn't moved much past second base, flirting with third. But the endless cuddling and making out was mind blowing, more than once

I had to stagger back to my dorm feeling hot and moist between my thighs.

I think secretly she reveled in the power she had over me by caressing my breasts over my shirt or applying pressure on my crotch with her legs. I would always wind up a whimpering ball of arousal who'd cave to her whims without a thought. But the braver I got, the more frequently I'd give as well as I got. I relished the occasions she would whisper, "tease" in my ear as she was whimpering in desire.

I had also gotten really close to her roommate Vicky in these past few weeks. Any time Valla and I weren't connected at the lips, the three of us would hang out. Shopping, talking, movies whatever. She was my second true friend now, and I loved every hyperactive inch of her as a sister. It was impossible not to grin like an idiot when you were around her contagious smile and enthusiasm.

True to her word, the next party Vicky attended she started a steamy makeout session on a couch with one of the female cheerleaders. She decided it was "awesome", and, "I told you I'd make a great lesbian!" Which made us laugh. She actually turned out to be more bisexual than anything as she still had no problems hooking up with occasional "cute" guy though she seemed to prefer the ladies.

People around campus were starting to call us the "three lez-migos" since we seemed to be an inseparable trio of friends. I'm not sure if it was meant to be an insult or not, but we kinda liked it.

One thing I learned quickly about Vicky, besides that she was a fierce friend, was that Valla wasn't exaggerating when she told me how intelligent Vicky really was. It seemed a dichotomy to me how someone so bubbly, hyper, and seemingly vapid could be so smart and insightful at the same time.

I was pleasantly surprised that here it was, the end of October and I had only had two additional episodes since the day I met Valla. I chalk that up to how much less stress and anxiety I have when I am around the girl I love. One episode was embarrassing, though, I was stressed about an exam in Psychology. I could feel it coming on and I tried to hold it off.

Fifteen minutes later I was shrugging my shoulder and repeatedly blurting out about the superego. Some of the students moved away from me to other seats, looking at me like I was a freak. I mouthed an apology to the silver-haired professor, Mr. Riser, during the whole thing. He was really cool about it. He never left his desk but just smiled up from his papers and nodded to me as I tried to control it while I worked on my exam.

Finally the twitching subsided and I pulled Little Vee out of my pocket and rubbed her with my thumb, calming myself just as I completed my exam. I hurried to the front of the class to hand in the paper, then turned quickly to leave in embarrassment.

Professor Riser caught my hand in a firm grip and turned me back, whispering, “Hey, it's okay.” He gave me a reassuring look and nod before releasing me. I avoided the stares from some of the other students as I left class.

The thought of that just fired off the memory of my first episode. I was knocked out of my thoughts by a sweet soprano voice asking, "SowhatdoyathinkMiadoeasn'tthatsoundcool?!" Vicky was literally bouncing on the bed in front of me where I was sitting between Valla's legs, laying back into her as she held my waist, rubbing her thumbs in circles on my exposed belly.

Valla snorted back a laugh behind me as I blinked at the little blonde dynamo in front of me. Luckily I have developed an internal decoder ring for Vicky's hyper babbling power. "Slow down Vickster, remember to put spaces between your words. Doesn't what sound cool?"

She stuck her tongue out at me then rolled her eyes and spoke slowly, enunciating each word like an English teacher. "I was saying that you and Valla should go as sexy vampires and I'll go as a sexy witch for the Halloween party at the Steam Plant Club or over at the Ballyhoo Club."

I was starting to feel anxious. "Why d-do all the costumes have to be s-sexy blondie?"

She laughed. "Well 'cause we ARE sexy. It isn't the fault of the costumes if they can't hide that."

I shook my head at her and couldn't help but smile at her enthusiasm. "No, I don't think so, I haven't even agreed to going to a Halloween party. I haven't gone to a party since that first one with Valla, they just make me too nervous."

Vicky looked past me to Valla, exaggerating her movement to look around me like I was as inconsequential as a shrub. Oh crap, she's not going to...

"Veeeee, can you puh-lease give me a hand convincing little miss party pooper here?"

Damn, she is. Vicky shot an evil smile toward me. Any protest I was about to make disappeared into the void along with any coherent thought, as a warm set of moist lips attached themselves to the pulse point on my neck from behind, kissing, nipping, and sucking.

My breathing was ragged and I'm sure my eyes were glazed over as Valla stopped her assault for a second. "Baby... I'd reeealy like to go the party. You'd make such a sexy vampire I wouldn't be able to keep my lips off of you. What do you say? Does that sound okay?" She continued her attack on my neck, causing me to gasp and nod my head repeatedly, unable to form words.

She stopped immediately and I could hear an evil chuckle in her voice as she spoke, "Good. How was that Vic? Now golly, where could we possibly locate some costumes on such short notice? The party is in just two hours."

I pressed my thighs tightly together in a sad attempt to quell my arousal. Vicky laughed at both the display and about how quickly I caved.

"Already picked them up last week, thank you for 'convincing' her Vee." She winked at us and hopped off the bed and ran to the closet.

I was still panting in want. "No fair..." I breathed out just to hear the two conspiring girls laughing at my sexual frustration. Valla lifted a hand to gently rub on my neck.

"Ooops. Sorry sweetie got too rambunctious here and marked my property."

I bit my lower lip, this wasn't the first time I sported a hickey from Valla and I hope to God it won't be the last. Her property indeed. I just snuggled back into her in response.

Vicky was back in front of us with three large white boxes, handing the first one to me. "One for you." Then one to Valla. "And one for you." She hugged the last box to her chest and ran to her bed. "And one for me!" She started stripping down on the spot to get into her costume, that girl possesses not a single ounce of modesty! I averted my gaze and blushed as she was already almost naked, then hopped off the bed, grabbed my purse, and headed to the bathroom with my box.

I opened the box and gasped. Inside was a gorgeous black and maroon velvet Victorian corset dress. I pulled everything out and checked the sizes. It was all in my size including the beautiful black stiletto heeled, calf high boots. It took longer than I thought to get dressed, both Valla and Vicky asked through the door if I needed any help as I slowly figured everything out. From the black, lingerie looking satin lace bra and panties to the thigh high black nylon stocking with garters this outfit was amazing.

I put on the ruffled blouse that went below the corset dress, noticing it was silk. I called out to Vicky as I was tightening the corset strings in the front, noticing how it raised my bust, making it more prominent, showing off way more cleavage than I am comfortable with. “Ummm... Vic, this outfit is gorgeous, it must have cost a fortune, I can't wear this.”

All I got in return was, “La, la, la, I can't hear you!”

I knew her family was rich, but she NEVER spoke of that and I have learned to never argue with her about it. I mean, who could possibly win a verbal argument with a chipmunk hopped up on caffeine? I smoothed my hands down the sides of the dress and opened one of the little boxes inside the larger box.

In it were some silver dangling clip on earrings with ruby red teardrop shaped crystals that looked like drops of sparkling blood. And a matching necklace on a delicate silver chain. I smiled at the fact that Vicky remembered that I didn't have pierced ears. Duh, she remembered, such is her curse. I had never had the need to look good before I had met Valla, so I had never got it done.

I put the jewelry on, then opened the next box to see two tiny porcelain white, pointed objects. I held one up, examining it. It was like a three-quarter cone with no back and a wire clip in the gap. From the front, it almost looked like a tooth. I almost facepalmed, realizing it was a fang. These weren't the cheap plastic, full mouth ones I remember from trick-or-treating in the first grade. They were single tooth works of art.

I slipped them over my upper canines and the wire held them firmly. I checked in the mirror and they looked like real fangs. I shrugged and sat on the edge of the tub to lace up the boots. Once I stood I took a few practice steps, and although I felt precarious on them I could smoothly navigate with them. I felt so tall.

I opened my purse and applied light eyeshadow but went a little heavy on the black eyeliner and dragged out the corners of my eyes to make them seem larger and more intense. There was knocking at the door again when I was applying my lipstick and gloss. “Just about finished!” I shouted.

Vicky whined back, “You've been in there over an hour Mi-mi! Come on!”

I finished up and fished Little Vee out of my pants pocket and placed her in my purse, then pulled on the long fingerless black lace gloves from the box. I grabbed my discarded clothing and my purse in one hand then turned to the full-length door mirror, stopping dead.

Holy shit! That's not me! I saw a pretty woman in the mirror. A pretty woman with fangs who looked scared to death. I yelled out to the girls, “I changed my mind, I can't do this. You two go ahead without me.”

Valla responded, “Oh no you don't, either come out now or I'm coming in Mia!”

I sighed. “Fine.”

I pushed my raven hair behind my shoulder and slowly opened the door, looking at the floor in total embarrassment as I stepped out. There was silence as I looked up to meet Valla's eyes. Her face was made up to look almost angelic with the counterpoint of the fangs that looked oddly sexy. Her mouth was hanging open. I couldn't see anything but her eyes at this moment as I searched them for approval.

“Holy shit!” I heard Vicky proclaim and I tore my eyes from Valla to look at the blonde. “You look…”

She was cut off by Valla's almost hoarse, whispering voice, “Fucking amazing!”

I turned back to her blushing more intensely than I ever had in my life.

That's when I saw more than just her face. My heart forgot how to beat and I inhaled sharply. I had never seen Valla look more beautiful, more stunning, more... sexy, than even in my wildest dream. Her outfit was the counterpoint to mine. Where mine had black, hers had maroon. Where mine had maroon, hers had black. Where I had silver jewelry, she had gold.

The dress showed off her feminine grace and her cleavage made me salivate. Her brown mane framed her face perfectly. Most striking were the stiletto boots that made her look even more delicate than I had ever seen, not to mention making her even taller.

We were broken out of our shared trance by Vicky huskily voicing, “Okay, I know what I'm fantasizing about the next time I masturbate. You two look like sex on heels.”

I gasped in embarrassment and Valla rolled her eyes at Vicky. “Remember Vickster, we discussed the topics of internal versus external dialog, and TMI?”

I heard Vicky giggle and I looked up and over at her, my eyes going wide. “Wow,” I said. “You clean up nicely Vic.” I grinned at her in her pure white witches costume with the barely there dress, white thigh high boots, and white classic witches hat. If there was such a thing as a sexy good witch, then there one was standing right there in all of its smiling blonde glory.

An irresistible force drew my hungry gaze back to the object of my affection, my eyes drinking her in from head to toe as I licked my lips subconsciously. Valla actually blushed under my scrutiny as I walked over and grabbed her hands in mine, leaned in and brushed our lips together so softly that if it wasn't for our lip gloss sticking together seductively as our lips parted I'm sure she would have been left wondering if we had actually kissed. Her eyes dilated as she let out the breath she was holding. “You are beauty personified Mia.” She licked her lips. I couldn't keep my eyes off of hers.

“Hey, horn dogs! Plenty of time to rip those costumes off each other later, let's get going to the party!” Vicky stated as she stepped between the two of us. Grabbing our hands and dragging us out the door. We both glanced at her and laughed as we marched through the quad toward Vicky's Range Rover. Before we got in the back seat, Valla whispered a one-word promise in my ear, "Tonight."

My knees went weak at the implication. Finally! There is a God!

We arrived at the Steam Plant Club and drove around the crowded parking lot a few times until we saw a car pull out. Vicky quickly zipped into it before anyone else could. We got out and checked each other out and proceeded toward the end of the long line of costumed party-goers waiting to get in just to be pulled by our hands by the freakishly strong tiny blonde witch toward the front of the line. "Where are you two going? Look in the mirror girls, we don't have to wait in no stinkin' line!"

Vicky was grinning like an idiot as we reached the door. She winked at the doorman who opened the velvet rope for us to go right in. We all shared a laugh, I was covering my mouth with my hand as Valla exclaimed over the loud dance music as we made our way toward the bar. "Oh my God! Vicky! How did you know he'd let us in like that? That was so surreal!"

She rolled her eyes at us. "Please ladies, you think you are the only ones drooling over each other? Oooooo I can use you two to get me into some other dance halls I've wanted to go to! OMG, you could sooo be like my golden club ticket! We could like..."

Valla cut her off. "Vicky, slow down. Breathe."

Vicky closed her mouth as we squeezed ourselves into some seats at the bar.

We ordered our drinks. Shots for the girls and a soft drink for me. The bartender didn't check their Ids even though we were all underage, but we didn't get the stamp on our hands at the door indicating that. Vicky gave me the car keys with a wink, knowing I'd be the designated driver.

Seconds later Vicky was yelling, “Redhead!” She walked away from us, threading her way through the crowd and sat on the lap of a cute redhead girl sitting at a table wearing a naughty schoolgirl costume. Within seconds, they were talking and laughing.

Valla shook her head at her, just as amazed as me about how easily Vicky could do that. Valla took a second shot of vodka and grabbed our three purses and handed them to the bartender. “Could you put these behind the bar for us please?” she asked, shooting him an innocent, pleading look. He did it happily. The next thing I knew, I was being dragged onto the dance floor by my sexy vampire goddess.

She whispered in my ear before we started dancing, “I've never seen you look so gorgeous. Tonight I'm finally going to taste you.” She had to support me as I got a little dizzy and my knees almost gave out. We started dancing together sexily, her behind me as we ground away while I bit my lower lip in want and arousal.

We were in our own world, nothing existed but each other. A couple songs later it switched to a slow song, Mandy Fay Harris'

'Oceans of Blue', and I glanced over toward Vicky to see her joined at the lips with the redhead. I smiled and turned my attention to Valla's eyes. They were full of compassion and lust as I draped my arms across her hips and she circled my neck with her own, pulling our faces an inch apart, foreheads touching.

She started kissing me as someone put their hand on my shoulder.

“Mind if I cut in?” The big guy with tight black curls asked as we pulled slightly away from each other.

Valla's eyes got steely as she said, “Sorry, I belong to her. And men aren't my type.”

He shot us both a sneer. “That's because you've never been with a real man.”

Valla tensed, my eyes were looking anywhere but at the man. “Well if you see one, send him on over.” she hissed then she kissed me passionately, returning us to our dance and leaving him standing there fuming for a few seconds before storming off.

“Sorry baby, just ignore that,” she whispered.

“O-o-okay.” I whispered back and melted into her for the rest of the dance. I felt so safe in her arms. As the night progressed, we wound up at the table with Vicky and her redhead, Molly. Molly's boyfriend had stormed off minutes after Vicky first arrived since Molly basically forgot about him with this oversexed white witch on her lap.

Valla and I had turned down many offers to dance from men and women, as we sat and chatted. We were snapped out of our personal conversation by Molly laughing and shouting at Vicky over the music. “No way girl. I'd so make you my bitch!”

Vicky looked like she was trying to contemplate something, but it was hard as she was way past the tipsy stage and well into drunk at this point. “O-M-G, you know what? I would sooo make an awesome submissive! I bet that would rock!”

Then before anyone could say anything, her eyes bulged and her hand went to her mouth as she stood up and staggered toward the restrooms.

“Oh, crap!” I exclaimed as I darted after her. This was not going to be pretty. We just barely got her into a stall and I held her hair back as she puked in the toilet.

After the dry heaves were over, she looked back at me and smiled. “Hi, Mia! I think I'm drunk.” Then she started giggling as I helped her up and to the sinks. After cleaning her up, I said, “Let's get you home before you turn into a pumpkin Vic.”

She smiled and said, “Okay. Hey, you're real pretty! You and Vee are so cute together.” She would have kept babbling, but it appeared she forgot what she was saying as we left the restroom.

Valla was already there with our purses and she grabbed Vicky's other side as we navigated out to the parking lot. I dug in my purse for the keys when I realized my hands were bare. “Oh, crap! Valla,

I left my gloves on Molly's table." She was already moving back toward the door, winking at me over her shoulder.

"I'll get em, be right back."

Vicky stood there inhaling the cool crisp air to clear her head a bit when someone shouted, "Hey fucking dykes!"

I looked over and two men and a woman were approaching us. One had a baseball bat.

"Steal my girl will you?"

I recognized the guy with the bat as Molly's 6'-4" boyfriend.

It all happened so fast. I was terrified as he raised the bat, my eyes darted around looking for an escape.

As he swung and hit Vicky in the arm, sending her to the asphalt he yelled, "Sinning pieces of shit like you are going straight to hell!"

She hit her head on the ground hard as the other two approached. I dove over Vicky, covering her body as I heard a crack and a sharp pain explode from my side where the bat connected with my ribcage.

I was screaming and sobbing, I knew I was going to die as I felt painful kicks and blows coming from multiple locations. I didn't want to die, I hadn't had my Valla yet! The last thing I saw as consciousness slipped from my grasp as I mumbled Valla's name was a stiletto heel connecting with the jaw of Molly's boyfriend.

Chapter 7 – Waking Up

I hurt, I knew something was wrong but couldn't do anything about it. I heard sounds and then nothing... blackness. Then light erupted and more sounds then blackness again. This went on forever. I swear I could hear Valla's voice, but I couldn't respond. Then blackness. I don't know how long this cycle continued. But through everything, the tones of Valla's voice kept popping up.

Then I was in the parking lot again. I was being beaten, but only one thought was going through my head. My eyes snapped open as I screamed, "VALLA!" My chest erupting in pain from the effort my eyes blinded by overhead lighting. I couldn't move. I hurt everywhere, someone immediately grabbed my right hand. I could feel the warmth spreading from the contact and could feel hot breath on my cheek.

Valla was sobbing into my ear over and over as I tried to focus. "Mia, I'm here... Mia. I was so scared baby. I'm here, I've got you."

I was lying down on something. A bed? Squinting, I turned my head and focused on Valla, tears were streaking her face as I saw people in white jackets streaming into the room saying stuff like, "She's finally awake!"

I was so tired. I smiled at the woman I loved, she looked so haggard. "Valla," I whispered as I lost my fight to stay awake and nodded off into sleep, the feel of her warm hand anchoring me.

When my eyes fluttered open again, I was still in a lot of pain but I could feel someone holding my hand. I turned my head painfully to see Valla in a chair beside me, grasping my hand as she slept. She looked like an angel. I scanned around, I was obviously in a hospital room. Every part of me hurt and I started to panic a bit, causing my heart rate monitor to beep much faster. This caused Valla's eyes to open and she glanced up at me and started to smile.

Before she could react, I remembered what had happened. I was so scared! My shoulder shrugged involuntarily up to my cheek and I screamed as the movement of my chest caused searing pain. “I never got to have her.” I blurted as my shoulder shrugged again. I saw white from the pain as I heard Valla yelling, “Nurse!” I twitched again and in agony yelled, “I never got her.” Other voices were now there, saying something I couldn't understand. I was reeling. Thankfully I passed out a couple twitches later whispering, “Never had her.”

I don't know how long I was out again when my eyes opened. It was mostly dark, just a single overhead near the door dimly lit the room. I knew I hurt every time I moved so I took stock of myself. I wiggled my fingers, my left arm ached. I wiggled my toes. So far so good. I tried to sit up, but the pain in my chest prevented it. I looked to my right and Valla stirred from her sleep in the chair beside my bed.

Her eyes lazily opened, meeting mine and she sat up suddenly, fully awake and smiling gently at me.

“There she is,” she spoke softly, grabbing my hand and lacing our fingers.

“Valhalla,” I whispered. I tried to sit up again, but she held me down.

“No baby, don't try to get up. You had me scared Mia.” She tenderly kissed my lips, which hurt, but it was worth it to have her lips on mine again. “Hang on a second, they told me to page if you woke up,” she said as she grabbed the call button laying on the bed beside me and pressed it, never releasing my hand with her other.

She gently moved some hair from my face and tucked it behind my ear as I heard something rolling in the hall up to my door. I studied Valla's face as a nurse wheeled in a computer on a little cart through the door. Valla's face was so gaunt, with hollow cheeks and dark circles under her eyes like she hadn't eaten or slept in a long time. But she was still beautiful, still my Valla. I smiled.

A hand was placed on Valla's shoulder and she looked back. The nurse motioned to the chair with her eyes. My girl whispered to me, “I'll be right here, I'm not going anywhere.” She kissed my forehead and released my hand and sat in the chair.

I missed the contact already. I looked at the older nurse. She smiled at me as she read my chart. “How are we feeling Miss Jacobs? Is your pain manageable, or would you like me to up your meds a bit?”

“I d-don't know. I just w-w-woke up. Am I okay?”

She looked at me with a touch of concern and asked, “Did you have this stutter before the... injures?”

I nodded and Valla added, “It's normal, she's just a little nervous.”

The nurse smiled at both of us. “Good. Okay. I'm going to look over your bandages and take some vitals. The doctor will be in soon to talk to you and give you a thorough checkup.”

She gently pulled down the sheet and opened my gown. I looked down and gasped. There were bandages taped on my chest below my breasts with a tube sticking out. What skin I saw was covered in multicolored bruises in various stages of healing and heart monitor pads. I finally noticed the cast on my left arm as she peeled up the chest bandage.

She prodded at some stitches and checked the bloody-looking liquid in the bag at the side of the bed that was connected to the tube. She placed a fresh bandage over the stitches and closed up my gown. She smiled at me. “That's looking much better. I'm sure the doctor will remove that soon.” She reached for my head and I flinched back. She moved her hands toward me again, slower. “It's okay hon. I'm just checking your bandages.”

I watched timidly as she peeled a bandage from the side of my head at the hairline and she just put it back in place without replacing it. “That's coming along nicely.” Then after prodding my cheek and lip, she pulled the sheet down further and checked the catheter I didn't realize was there. “The doc should let you start getting up in a couple days and we can get this thing out. I know how uncomfortable these can be." She offered a sympathetic smile as she pulled the sheet back up under my arms.

She typed a few things on the computer cart then walked to my right side and pulled up my sleeve to check my IV and take my pulse and blood pressure. After entering that information, and the readings from the various pieces of equipment she asked, "I'm sure you are thirsty, we can start you out on ice chips to see if you can keep stuff down if you'd like."

I nodded and she grabbed a little plastic cup of ice chips off the cart and placed them on a napkin on the table that swung from the bed with a little plastic spoon.

"I'll be back later to check in on you." She looked over at Valla then said to me with a smile, "You got a hell of a girl there."

I just smiled and nodded enthusiastically. "I do."

She assured me that the doctor would be in soon and then I should get some sleep, and told the same to Valla.

The moment she left Valla was back by my side grasping my hand, feeding me her strength and warmth. I felt a tear rolling down my cheek. "I was so scared I wasn't going to see you again when they were attacking me last night."

She gently wiped the tear from my cheek with the thumb of her free hand. "Shhh... It's okay. I'm right here. Nobody is taking you away from me. Ever. And baby, it was seven days ago. You were in a coma for four days, then after your Tourette episode they put you in a medically induced coma for anther two days to let your body recover more without you doing more damage."

"You've been here the whole time?" I asked quietly.

She smiled. "Every day until they kick me out at night. But Nurse Carol there has started letting me sneak in and spend the night." She grinned at her own conspiracy. I chuckled and gasped, it hurt. Valla winced at my gasp. "I was so scared baby. I'm so glad you are going to be okay. I really couldn't live without you."

I smiled weakly, it was my turn to reassure her. "You are never going to lose me, Valla."

I looked at our hands and then scowled as I raised our hands up to look at her's. Her knuckles were all bruised and scabbed.

"What happened?" I rasped out as she held a spoon of ice chips in front of me with her other hand. I took them in my mouth, they felt divine melting and moistening my mouth.

"It's nothing Mia," she whispered.

I opened my mouth like a baby bird and she delivered another spoonful of ice. I let them melt in my mouth. Swallowing the resulting water hurt a little, but the cool sensation going down my throat felt good. Just then a balding, portly doctor walked in followed by a very buff looking police officer.

The kindly looking doctor smiled at me. "Nice to have you with us finally Miss Jacobs. I'm Dr. Tanner. You had us worried for a bit. I'm going to do a quick checkup then this officer would like to ask you a few questions if you are feeling up to it." He smiled again as I nodded.

Valla moved out of his way but being sure to stand where I could see her. She grounded me. He went to work checking everything the nurse did, and wrote some stuff on my chart and slid the drain out of my chest. "We won't be needing that anymore."

After finally shining his penlight in my eyes he said, "Do you remember what happened? I nodded, and he said, "Good. Now would you like to know about your injuries?" I nodded again as Valla moved back to my side, grasping my hand as he spoke, "In the attack, you suffered five broken ribs. A punctured lung, multiple contusions to around 40% of your body. A broken left ulna. A dislocated left shoulder. A swollen ankle. And a hairline fracture of the skull."

I'm sure I looked appalled. He smiled compassionately.

"But the good news is you will be out of here in a few days and after about eight weeks of recovery you should be able to play the piano again."

I looked at him, "B-but I d-don't play the piano."

He looked amused. "Drat, I thought I was just THAT good of a doctor."

I couldn't help but smile.

He wrapped up telling me to get some rest after the officer was done with me and looked back and forth between Valla and I. "Goodnight Miss Jacobs, Miss Taylor."

We both bid him good night then the officer stepped up to the bed and visibly winced when he looked at me.

"Hello Miss Jacobs, you feel up to answering a few questions?" he asked. Then looked at Valla "Alone?"

I grabbed Valla's hand hard. "Can she p-please stay?" I almost whispered.

He looked between us then said "Okay but..." he turned to Valla, "No coaching."

She nodded and remained silent.

"Can you tell me in your own words the events that led up to your attack?"

I nodded and began as Valla rubbed her thumb on the back of my hand. "Valla, Vicky a-and I were at a Halloween p-party at the Steam Plant Club and Vicky got a little s-sick. So we left to t-t-take her home. I had forgotten my gloves at the t-table so Valla went b-back in to get them while we waited at th-the car."

I closed my eyes fighting off tears at the next part. "S-someone started yelling bigoted things at Vicky and I. It was two g-guys and a girl. One was Molly's b-boyfriend. He had a bat."

The officer stopped me and held up three photographs. "Are these the people?"

I nodded "Y-yeah. The middle one is Molly's boyfriend. The other t-two I don't know, but that is them."

He nodded and wrote something down and looked at me to continue. I took a deep breath and released it quickly from the sharp pain in my chest from taking it. I took shallower breaths. "He hit Vicky w-with the bat!" I was crying now then my eyes shot wide. "Vicky! I-is she okay!?" I looked at Valla urgently.

She nodded. "She's fine baby."

I sighed in relief. "She d-didn't move after she hit the ground. I was s-so scared I t-tried to protect her... they all just kept hitting me and kicking me and hitting me." I was almost yelling. Valla squeezed my hand and I squeezed my eyes shut. "Then I woke up here," I whispered.

He finished writing and then looked at me with a gentle smile. "Thanks, Miss Jacobs, I got all we need. We have the guy with the bat in another room here, almost in as bad of shape as you and bystanders helped detain the girl. But the third guy is in the wind. We know who he is and will grab him when he resurfaces. We will be treating this as a hate crime. The ignorance of people never ceases to astound me. Hopefully, more activists like that Anabella West girl down in Vancouver can start educating people. We'll be in touch." Then his voice softened, "Get better soon okay?"

I nodded as he left.

I looked at Valla and she placed a gentle kiss on my lips. "Get some sleep now baby."

I smiled at her. "What did he mean Molly's boyfriend is in another room in as bad of shape as me?"

She just shook her head. "Nothing Mia, it's not important. Get some sleep."

She sat there holding my hand as sleep crept up on me, my last thought was of how warm and safe her hand made me feel.

Chapter 8 – Home To The Dorm

The next morning I sent Valla to the cafeteria to get something to eat, she looked positively anorexic! I was getting worried. She couldn't tell me the last time she had eaten.

A couple minutes after she left the room I was already feeling a little anxious. Then I heard a gentle knocking at the door. "Come in," I said quietly. In walked a tiny smiling blonde with a pink cast on her arm and a pink bandage over her eye.

"Vicky!" I said enthusiastically. I was so glad she really was okay! She winced when she looked at me. I looked at her. "Why does everyone do that? Do I look that bad?" I asked as I shoveled some ice chips in my mouth. I was getting so hungry.

She smiled brightly at me and almost skipped up to the bed and grabbed my hand between hers. "No, even beat up and bruised you make it look good." She grinned, wiggling her eyebrows.

I chuckled. "Ow, ow, ow."

She mouthed, "I'm sorry."

I shrugged a little, smiling at her.

"So, like, you are officially my hero. What the hell were you thinking shielding me like that?" She shot an accusatory glare at me.

I looked at her sheepishly. "Nobody hurts my friends. All two of them." I tried not to laugh as she giggled.

She got a conspiratorial look on her face and leaned in. "Well, old bat puss won't try that again for a very long time after the hurt Vee put on him."

I was a little confused. "What do you mean?"

Her eyes widened "You don't know? Well when Vee returned with your gloves to see those... those... people... attacking you while you covered me, she cut down Molly's ex, Max, like she was was a lumberjack. She was wailing on him and kicking him so violently on the ground that it took three bystanders to pull her off of him. She was screaming about Max not touching 'her girl.' She fucked him up bad."

She smiled with pride at that, I was amazed that the love of my life could take on a big guy like that. That seemed so... I don't know, sexy?

Vicky continued, "Some girl, Missy Hannigan, was on her way into the Plant when she saw what was going on and jumped the girl that was kicking you. She beat the shit out of her and held her till the police showed up."

I was in shock. Missy Hannigan? Of all the people in the world, she helped me?

"Oh!" she exclaimed as she pulled a red permanent marker out of her pocket. "Can you sign my cast? I'll sign yours! It's like we are twins! 'Cept yours is white and mine is pink. Oh my Gawd, I'd make a friggin' awesome twin. We could be all..."

I interrupted, “Vickster! Slow down. Breathe.” I grinned and took the marker from her as she smiled and held her arm out to me.

Her pink cast was covered in red hearts and signatures, a large one caught my eye, 'Get better soon! XOXO Molly', with a heart surrounding it. I quirked an eyebrow, pointing the marker at it and Vicky wiggled her eyebrows. I laughed, I hurt, and I signed. She took the marker and ran around the bed and started working on signing mine as she spoke.

“So when do you get to go home and junk? We miss you and Vee around. She's all obsessively here all the time, all protect-y and stuff. I'm surprised she's not here right now.” She raised an eyebrow and winced since it was by her bandage.

I chuckled softly so I wouldn't cause myself pain. “They say I can go home in a few days. I sent Valla to the cafeteria to eat. It looks like she has been starving herself. Promise you will help to fatten her up.”

She brightened up at the request. “You got it! Can I ask a weird question?”

I looked at her and squinted a little. “Ummm... sure?”

She leaned in a bit as she continued working on my cast. “I've always meant to ask. Why do you keep calling her Valla when her name is Vee? And like why have I NEVER heard you call her Vee? She snapped at me, saying that only you could call her Valla when I said it once. Is like, Vee short for something?”

Remembering my first conversation with Valla, I nodded and crooked my finger at her to come in closer. She leaned in with an excited look like I was going to share a secret with her. Then I whispered, “It's short for her name.” Then I chuckled. “Ow.”

She slapped my shoulder. “Oh, she's so right! You ARE a tease!”

We shared a smile just as Valla wandered in shoveling chocolate pudding into her mouth. She put it down on my swivel table. “Hi Vic!” she said cheerily as she pulled a sealed cup of lime jello out of her pocket and put it on the table with a spoon and opened it. “The nurse said you could try some jello and see if it stays down Mia. I had to track your favorite down. Finally found lime!”

I smiled at the fact she remembered one of our late night conversations where I had mentioned it.

Vicky finished with what she was doing on my cast and put the marker in her pocket, then swiped a finger through Valla's pudding.

“Hey!” Valla exclaimed. “Thief! Now you'll get Vee germs.”

Vicky laughed at that. “Oooo, so it's like we kissed then! My first Vee kiss! Mmmm... Your kisses are like chocolate!” We all laughed at that.

“Ow.” I slowly raised my arm, suffering pain in the shoulder and chest but couldn't see what she put on the underside of the cast very well. “What's it say?”

Valla stood and walked around to look as I started shoveling lime jello into my mouth.

Oh my Gawd, real food!

I stopped pigging out when Valla snorted.

I looked over "What?"

She grinned at me. "Well in a plethora of little hearts it says 'Get better soon Mia, the 'three lez-migos' miss you! Victoria Davenport', followed by some hugs and kisses." They both laughed as the blood drained from my face.

"I'll be stuck with that for weeks until I can take it off!" I was stressing for a second until Valla slipped Little Vee into my hand with a wink.

The next couple days went the same way. I was on solid food finally and the catheter was out. I painfully had to be helped up to standing five times a day and shuffled over to the restroom in my room on a crutch to relieve myself. Did I mention painfully?

Finally, the doctor came in and told me I was ready to be released. He went through all the instructions for home recovery and care for the wounds. He prescribed pain medication, antibiotics, and at least five days more of bed rest as well as weekly office visits to assess my recovery from my surgery and mending bones. Valla swore she would dutifully take care of all of it.

It was at this point that I asked the doctor quietly, "Umm... I'm not sure my student health insurance will cover everything. Can the hospital set me up with a payment plan or an assistance program to help out with the bill?"

I wasn't quiet enough because before he could speak, Valla chimed in, “Nonsense, I'll handle it. It won't even put a dent in my inheritance.”

Dr. Tanner flipped through some pages. “Actually, your care, including all follow-ups, has been paid in full by Frank and Maira Davenport, the parents of the girl you protected.”

Valla and I exchanged shocked glances. Valla helped me get dressed and a nurse came after we got a call from Vicky saying she was downstairs. I was loaded up into a wheelchair and wheeled out to the waiting Range Rover. After throwing the crutch in it was a comedy of errors between the three of us to get me loaded up into the car without too much pain.

Valla coughed a couple times before getting in beside me. Then it was off to “Home”, or in my case Valla and Vicky's dorm room or the VV Lair as we all started calling it.

We sat down, ordered pizza, and relaxed finally. Time suddenly slowed to a normal pace after the whirlwind of my hospital days. Valla coughed, then cleared her throat and we all sat on her bed to wait for the food. I carefully laid down to get more comfortable, my head in Valla's lap with her stroking my hair.

Vicky was the first to break the three-way smiling contest, for once her voice held a serious tone. “It's so great to see you home and safe Mia.”

Valla smiled down on me and gave me a tender upside down kiss on my lips. “I second that,” she grinned, causing me to parrot her grin.

Vicky whispered, “Just how cute are you two?” She snapped like the ten-millionth picture of us since she met us.

Valla reached down with one hand to grasp my good hand, interlacing our fingers as we all discussed everything from how we were going to catch up on our coursework to how this was going to work with the three of us in one room until I recover enough to be on my own in my dorm again.

After we had gorged ourselves on pizza and soda it was extremely late, the two girls had class in the morning. Before I knew it, I heard tiny snores and looked down to see Vic asleep across my legs, hugging my left calf. Valla moved from behind me to beside me and cuddled into my good side. And just stared into my eyes.

I don't know what came over me, but my eyes watered up and I whispered to Valla, “I love you.” A tear did escape her eye.

“I love you too,” she whispered back. She looked happy and amazed at the same time. “Wow. So that's what it's like? The deafening whisper.”

I didn't understand but I didn't care, we had finally spoke the words we were longing to hear. They echoed in my head as I dropped into the first peaceful slumber I had had in over a week.

Chapter 9 – Valla's Confession

I woke up to Valla coughing in the bathroom. Vicky was nowhere to be seen, she had probably already gone to breakfast. Valla wandered out in some boxer shorts and a t-shirt and stopped shyly when she saw me admiring her.

"Did my coughing wake you baby? I'm sorry," she said, offering me a small smile.

I frowned. "It's fine. I'm worried about you, you spread yourself too thin taking care of me at the hospital."

She shook her head slowly as she responded, "It's just a tickle in my throat. I'll be fine. Now let me go do something about breakfast for you before I have to go to class." She walked over and handed me my pills and a bottle of water to wash them down with. I did it with a silly grin on my face. She was so hawt when she was taking care of me.

She caught my hungry appraisal of her, as I bit my lower lip. "Hey now. None of that until we can both do something about it you tease." She grinned with a predatory look as she leaned down into a heated kiss. Then she pulled back, smiling bigger leaving my lips parted with want.

I was frustrated. "Who's the tease now?" We both laughed, then I remembered something I had wanted to ask her.

"You said something about a deafening whisper last night. What did you mean by that?" I asked, cocking an eyebrow.

Her eyes glittered with love and happiness as she replied, “Well, a deafening whisper once spoken is a defining moment in time where two lives are changed irrevocably whether for the good or the bad. Just as our whispers last night changed us forever. Not only am I yours but I want to be yours forever.”

My eyes were getting misty, she made me so happy! And speaking like that just brought my happiness to a whole new level. I was about to speak when she bit her lower lip seductively. “Hurry up and get better, I made you a promise the night of the party and I aim to keep it.”

I remembered her flirty promise and gasped. “Damn you!” I said. “No fair getting me aroused when I can't do anything about it!”

She leaned in for another teasing, lingering kiss before moaning and turning for the door. “Be right back with foodage baby... I love you!”

I swooned and yelled back as the door was closing, “I love you too!”

I got up and grabbed my crutch then hobbled my way into the bathroom and got ready for yet another exciting day of forced bed rest. I rolled my eyes at the prospect. I had already gone stir crazy at the hospital, this was going to be just as bad. It was only Wednesday and I wouldn't be able to get back to the real world until Monday!

I looked at my bruised face in the mirror. The bruises looked awful, turning a sickly brown and yellow as they were healing. At least most of the swelling had gone down around my eye and lip. The cuts were scabbed up and healing quite nicely. I couldn't change my clothes without a good deal of pain, so I decided to stay in my bed clothes. I'm helpless!

After getting cleaned up the best I could, I hobbled back to the bed, my chest aching from the movement. I grabbed one of my course books and Little Vee and started catching up on the two weeks I'd been out of commission. But my mind kept drifting back to the attack, I was so scared.

I had to go through that simply because I loved a girl. Why the hell are some people filled with so much hate? It seems the only thing I ever did to them was to simply exist. My thoughts were interrupted when my goddess came back in the room with some breakfast burritos and a couple of coffees.

I placed my book back on the stack, pushing it around and nudging it with my finger until it was lined up perfectly. Valla coughed a little, and we ate. She noticed me stuffing Little Vee back in my pants, and she smiled. “You sure you are okay Valla? That cough sounds awful,” I asked, concern tinging my voice.

She grinned softly back at me. “Never been better, let's concentrate on you getting better.”

She gave me a tantalizing kiss and started toward the door before I called out to her, “Valla. Could you... umm... help me get changed? I couldn't get out of these damn clothes.” I looked down in embarrassment.

She crossed back over to me and put a finger on my chin, raising my eyes to hers. I'll never get enough of the feline look of her eyes, punctuated with those darker flecks of amber. “Of course baby.”

We had difficulty getting the oversized t-shirt off without causing too much pain, so we decided blouses were the way to go. She selected one of hers from her closet. I could button them without problems though twisting to bring the shirt around my shoulders was still out of my current pain threshold capability.

She kissed the bare skin of my shoulders, causing a delightful warmth to bloom throughout my body as she wrapped my shoulders in the blouse. It smelled of Valla. I inhaled shallowly, wishing I could take deeper breaths of her intoxicating scent without hurting my ribs.

I dropped my pants in a happy daze and stepped out of them. She grabbed another pair from my bag beside the bed I tried to bend to pull them up, but I couldn't bend much beyond my waist without pain overriding me. “God, I'm helpless,” I said, shaking my head as Valla bent to check my ankle wrap then pull the pants up my legs stopping to kiss the skin of my thighs before I grabbed the tops of them and pulled them over my hips, breathing raggedly as I zipped and buttoned them. “Tease!” I muttered huskily.

“No... payback.” She grinned and gave me a quick peck on the lips. “Gonna be late to class. See you here at lunch. Vickster will be checking in between classes too. Love you!” Before I could respond she was out the door like a giggling whirlwind. Leaving me alone and aroused. Back to my studies.

Over the next couple days, Valla's cough was getting worse and even Vicky was getting on her case about getting it checked out. She kept insisting that the first priority was getting me healthy again. Vicky and I would exchange worried glances.

Saturday morning rolled around and I woke up to Valla sitting on the edge of the bed coughing violently. She pulled her hand from her mouth when she saw that I was awake, I noticed something and I grabbed her hand and looked at it. There was blood on it. “Valla! We are going to the hospital, now!” I exclaimed, glaring at her for not letting on how serious this was getting.

She was opening her mouth to protest when Vicky sat up in her bed. “What's going on?”

I looked over at her. “Get the car Vic, we need to get Valla to the doctor, now!” Without a word, she jumped out of bed and threw on some clothes. Walking over to the dresser and throwing clothes at Valla.

My girl opened her mouth to protest again but wound up coughing instead. Then she just lowered her eyes to the floor and started getting dressed. There was a shirt in my face, I grabbed it from Vicky as she started peeling off the sleeping shirt I had on. As I was buttoning up the shirt, she was already sliding some pants up my legs. I was stunned, she was a calm machine!

I hobbled up onto my crutch as she rummaged through the pants I had worn yesterday, retrieving Little Vee, and handing her to me. She grabbed Valla by the shoulders and started leading her out to the car. I hobbled after them.

There wasn't much talking on the way to the hospital, Valla instructed Vicky to go to a different clinic instead. We both kept looking at Valla, not wanting to ask. I was getting so worried. I felt... No. Not now. I started fighting off an episode. By the time we arrived, I was wringing my hands in the effort of staving it off.

Valla was pale and kind of out of it, but Vicky glanced at me and she noticed. I'm sure my face was strained with the effort. I had to let loose, but I couldn't, not until Valla was checked in. I needed release. I was sweating badly.

We got to the reception desk and with one look at Valla the receptionist exclaimed, “Miss Taylor! I'll call Dr. Townsend right away.” Valla nodded and the receptionist turned to Vicky. “Just bring her back to the second door on the right. The doctor will be in in a minute,” the woman said, already lifting the receiver to her ear.

If I had been thinking straight at that time, I would have realized that Valla must come here frequently. They knew exactly who she was and didn't ask any questions about what was going on. I numbly followed them into the exam room. I was in phantom pain, restraining myself, fighting hard not to explode.

A nurse met us in the room with what was apparently Valla's chart which Vicky made a point of keeping her eyes away from. She didn't want the information burned into her brain.

As soon as Valla was lying on a bed with the nurse taking her vitals, Vicky was grabbing my arm and quickly dragging me out of the room. “We'll be right back,” she said calmly to the nurse as we passed by. I followed her wobbling on my crutch numbly until we arrived at a restroom in the corridor.

She pulled the door open then stuck her head in. After pulling back, she gave my arm a gentle squeeze and pushed me into the room shutting the door behind me.

The moment the door shut I blurted, “Fuck!” My shoulder spasmed to my cheek with a vengeance. I almost fell off my crutch. I sat on the toilet seat and just let my body do whatever it wanted. “Fuck!” The spasms were violent after being denied for so long, but I could feel the tenseness draining with each one. “Fuck it!” I felt relief.

I heard Vicky telling someone in the corridor, “She's fine. I got this.”

I was crying now, riding out the waves as they slowly subsided. Finally Vicky cracked the door open and looked at me, then walked in, locking the door behind her and watching my last couple shoulder shrugs.

“Hey,” she said cheerfully with a big smile, handing me a tissue. “You ready to go see your girl?”

After drying my eyes, I struggled to my feet. I looked in the mirror. Well, at least I couldn't look any worse with my bruised up face. I looked to Vic and whispered, “Thank you.”

She looked at me and shrugged. “What? This?” She waved it off. “You're the dumbass that fought it off so long.” She winked and I almost laughed. She's only the second person ever to not show pity over my condition. No quarter asked, no quarter given. She smiled and opened the door and ushered me out.

We got to Valla's room and I peeked in the door, she was listening to the doctor as she was huffing on a nebulizer. I looked back to Vicky and she put a hand on my shoulder and gave a gentle squeeze as she spoke, “I'll be in the waiting room.” I watched her leave, then hobbled my way into the room, putting a smile on my face for Valla.

She took the nebulizer out of her mouth long enough to say, “Hey baby.”

I grinned at her, trying to hide my concern. “Hey, yourself,” I replied. I looked at the doctor. “H-how's my girl doing?”

He glanced over at Valla and she nodded slightly in permission before he spoke, “Well, Miss Taylor is just having another nasty bout with walking pneumonia. Looks like she waited quite a long time to come in this time.”

This has happened before? I felt guilty that she ignored it to watch over me and mumbled to him, “S-she was taking care of me. I should have m-made her come in sooner.”

He looked at us and his demeanor softened. “Well, no harm, no foul THIS time,” he said then looked at her accusingly. “Stop being so stubborn when it comes to your treatment,” he chastised as he removed the nebulizer and started writing things on her chart, and took her vitals again.

“Sorry Doc.,” she said like a little kid who had just got caught stealing cookies.

I looked at her, picking my words carefully. “What's wrong with you Valla. You have to tell me.” She looked at me, her lips pursed tightly shut and looking at the doctor pleadingly.

He apparently understood her implied consent and turned to me. “Vee here is just having another nasty round with her cystic fibrosis.” He placed a hand on my shoulder and squeezed gently before he walked toward the door, calling back to Valla, “A nurse will be in in a minute to get you your prescriptions, and have you fill out some paperwork.”

I was still standing there stunned and unmoving. Cystic fibrosis? Isn't that terminal? What, like a 25-30 year life expectancy? My eyes were watering up. I turned to her and she looked... ashamed? She wouldn't meet my eyes.

“When we get back, we need to talk,” she whispered hoarsely. I just nodded and went to where she was sitting on the edge of the bed, I joined her silently and laid my head on her shoulder to wait for the nurse.

With the prescriptions in hand and an order of two days bed rest and warned to take it easy for at least two weeks more we picked up Vicky doing every crossword in the magazines in the waiting room at the same time, and we were off.

The ride back to the VV Lair was silent, with me cuddled into Valla. Vicky knew not to talk. She had been amazing all day. If I hadn't been so worried about my girl, I probably would have wondered how she was able to turn off her hyperactive personality at the proper times.

Back in the room we laid down in bed, Vicky making an excuse to leave us alone to talk. Something about bringing back chicken soup for healing all of us up. I turned to Valla on my good side and she turned so that we were face to face, inches apart with my hand in hers.

I looked at her and asked with pain in my voice, "Cystic fibrosis?"

She nodded and responded, "Sorry I never said anything, that I hid it. I just wanted to be with you without that hanging over us."

I was tearing up as I choked out, "But... I want to be with you forever."

She reached up to my cheek, stroking it gently with her thumb as she whispered, "I never expected to meet you. I never expected to fall madly in love with you. I never expected US... and then WE happened. Then I couldn't tell you. I couldn't bear to see you hurt. I just didn't know what to do. I thought I'd lose you if I revealed it."

She tore her eyes from mine and looked down at our hands. A million questions were going through my mind, but one dominating the rest. I whispered, “How much longer?”

I reached over with my cast and brought her gaze back to mine, lifting her chin with my finger as she replied, “Two, maybe three years... I hope to finish college before...”

We were both silently crying now. “But... it's not fair,” I whispered. She shook her head in agreement. I took a gasping breath, “Am I yours?”

She nodded.

“Are you mine?” My emerald eyes searched her amber as she nodded again. “Then it's enough. Can I have every moment?” I chocked out. She nodded again and buried her head in the crook of my neck and I held her as she sobbed herself to sleep.

I numbly sat there and just watched her breath. God, I love her. I took a deep breath, ignoring the pain in my ribs from doing so, and forced my tears to stop. It was at that moment that I resolved that I was going to fill every day, every moment with her for as long as we had with nothing but love. I would not be weak, I would be strong for her, for us. I kissed the top of her head and waited for Vicky to return.

About an hour later Vicky returned with chicken noodle soup and soft drinks. I gently woke up Valla and we all sat around on the bed, taking turns with the big spoons, dipping into the huge communal bowl of soup.

Vic's bubbly personality had returned with a vengeance, keeping us all smiling and laughing the rest of the weekend. She knew it was needed. We all had an unspoken agreement that we would hold off a bit before any serious talks. Right now it was about being together and healing.

Molly stayed in the VV Lair on Sunday night and they made some suggestive squeaking noises most of the night over on Vic's bed when they thought we were asleep. Valla and I had to fight back our giggles.

Chapter 10 – Planning the Future

Monday morning rolled around and Molly was nowhere to be seen. Valla and I were officially off of bed rest. I can actually go to class today! I was able to actually dress myself with great difficulty after my shower. I must be recovering. Valla made it difficult for me to focus as she combed out my hair for me, leaving hot wet kisses all over the exposed skin of my neck.

I made sure Little Vee was in my pocket and we headed out the door. My ankle was feeling pretty good today, only a couple more days with the crutch and I should be able to walk fine without it. We made our way to one of the cafeterias for breakfast, with Valla and Vicky carrying my books and purse. How pathetic am I?

“See if you can't snag an open table ladies and I'll go order us some grub,” Valla said with a quick kiss, leaving my lips parted, wanting more.

As we turned toward the tables, I bumped into someone. “S-sorry,” I said and stopped when I realized who it was. “S-sorry Missy,” I repeated looking at the floor.

She looked me up and down, cringing at my face a bit. “Not a problem,” she said quickly as she turned to walk off.

“Wait!” I called after her.

She stopped with her back still to me but didn't turn around. Vicky was looking back and forth between the two of us in confusion. I quietly said, “Thanks for helping to s-save me.”

Missy took a deep breath then turned around, her expression was unreadable as she said coolly, “You're still a spaz.”

Then her face and voice softened, she reached out and placed a hand gently on my arm. “But nobody deserves this.” Gesturing at the condition I was in with her head. Then she turned and walked off, her voice cold again, saying over her shoulder, “Get better soon freak.”

Vicky and I looked at each other and Vic chirped, “My, she's certainly warm and fuzzy.” We both cracked up as Valla arrived behind us, bearing three breakfast burritos and coffee on a tray. I swear we're going to turn into breakfast burritos one day. But that's not a bad thing is it? They are so yummy!

“What I miss?” my girl asked cutely as we sat at the table. I started unwrapping a burrito as I spoke to her, her eyes twinkling with mischief.

“That was Missy, she was almost a human being today, but Vickster isn't too convinced.”

We all shared a smile and devoured our meal. I found it surreal that we were all recovering from something or another. Then all rational thought left me as I ate when a warm hand rested on my knee, Valla faking a little Miss Sweet and Innocent look as she ate one handed.

My first class was spent with the teaching assistant to my professor, getting assignments and new due dates to catch up with the rest of the class. Then it was back to the VV Lair until after lunch. I was excited to get back to art class. Just as excited when Valla gave me a steamy, toe-curling kiss at the door when she dropped me off there.

Mrs. Sax, I mean Jenny came motoring over quickly, wincing when she saw my face. I'm really getting tired of that, why can't I just wear my hoodie until I heal?

“Mia, they really put the hurt on you, didn't they?” she half asked half stated, concern was etched on her face.

I smirked. “You should see the other guy's bat, my face really did a number on it!” She didn't smile. I thought I was funny.

She dismissed our conversation and excitedly changed the topic. “Well I have news for you, do you want to talk about it now or at the end of class?”

I looked over at her as I grabbed a couple large stacks of felt sheets in various colors. I was starting to get suspicious about all the new materials popping up close to my workstation. I set a piece of cardboard in front of me and started cutting the felt into tiny, quarter-inch triangles. “I can talk as I work. It's better that way, then I don't obsess so much.”

She watched my hands go as I paid more attention to her than what I was doing as she spoke. “Well that first work that you let me submit into the National Collegiate Competition in New York City won first place, and you have an offer on that piece from a private collector there! Forty thousand dollars if you are interested. Otherwise they will ship it back here.”

I was shocked, someone thought my art was worth something? "Ummm... okay. Wow."

She smiled and nodded. "Okay, I'll get it set up for you. There were also inquiries about commissioning some works, I'll forward the info to your email." She was beaming proudly at me.

We spoke about the details and the upcoming student gallery art auction at the end of the month. I started building little towers assembling four different colored triangles to make tiny square layers. Then stacking multiple layers in a predetermined pattern until each little tower glued to the cardboard till they were six inches tall.

As we spoke, I continued making towers and staggering them at various, seemingly random points on the cardboard. Jenny started to get distracted and seemed more interested in what I was doing than talking. I finished our conversation by saying, "Class is almost over."

She glanced at the clock on the wall behind me, confirming my internal chronometer. "Two minutes to go," she breathed.

"Done!" I said.

She looked over my creation with a confused look on her face, it apparently didn't look like anything to her. I smiled and pointed at her feet, she nodded and sat put as I walked across the room a ways and placed the sheet with the felt towers down on her desk.

"Squat so your eyes are even with your desktop," I instructed. A couple of the other students had moved to her side and they all squatted. A communal gasp was uttered. “On my God!” Jenny breathed. Then I turned the work on her desk to the next side.

“Unbelievable” someone said as I turned it again to the third side then the fourth.

I knew what they were seeing. One side, when lined up, made a very pixelated illusion of my dog Noodles from when I was four. One side had the word 'Love' because I was thinking of Valla at the time, the next was the wagon I had as a young child. Last was the word 'Unfair' because again I was thinking of Valla.

I walked back over to my workstation with the piece and slid it on the upper shelf above the bench. Jenny still hadn't said anything else, she just stared at me as I hobbled toward the door on my crutch, happy that with a single idea I was able to make four works. That was fun!

I leaned against the wall in the corridor to wait. I caught the scent of vanilla moments before the soft hands covered my eyes. I smiled from ear to ear as I turned around directly into a hug from Valla. “Hey! You're supposed to guess who!” She laughed.

I acted nonchalant. “I'm just in the habit of hugging anyone who does that to me.” I teased as I released our hug. She pulled me back into her possessively.

“Better not be anyone else stealing hugs from you,” she whispered in my ear, nipping at my earlobe.

We giggled at each other and made our way to my psychology class where she bid me farewell. Just ninety minutes till I get to see her again! Five thousand four hundred seconds. I started counting in my head. This was going to be a long class.

Eventually, I made it through the day and Vicky met me at class to take my books instead of Valla. I looked at her with curiosity as she took my books and we started walking. “Where's Valla?” I glanced over at the super-peppy blonde.

She shrugged. “She texted me to see if I could get ya back to the Lair. Something about her English Lit professor needing to talk to her.” We were half way through the Quad when she stopped walking.

She stood there staring straight ahead, her perpetual smile was gone, not looking at me and asked in a husky voice, “It's bad isn't it?” My breath caught, I knew she was referring to Valla's condition. I had been trying so hard to be strong, but I broke down right there on the spot.

Small, strong arms were suddenly around me, pulling me into a hug and I sobbed into Vicky's shoulder. I let myself cry, it felt good to release it. I'll never let myself break like this in front of my Valla, she needs me to be strong.

I choked back the tears and took a cleansing breath as Vicky stroked my hair with one hand. As we pulled apart from the hug I whispered, “Thank you Victoria.”

She looked into my eyes to comfort me. “Hey, everyone needs a good cry sometimes. Let's get you back to the Lair to wait for your girl.” Her smile brightened her face again as we continued our journey, and as always it was contagious as I found myself smiling too. I was feeling much better after that emotional purge.

We were sitting on Valla's bed playing slap jack when she walked in with a grin plastered on her face. She stole a line from Vicky as she skipped up to us. “One for you!” She kissed Vic on the top of her head. “And one for you!” She put me in such a passionate lip lock that it literally stole my breath away. I was gasping somewhere on cloud nine as she slid herself behind me and circled my waist with her warm arms, her marvelous scent enveloping me as she peered over my shoulder.

I turned my head and gave her a quick peck on the lips as coherent thought returned. I bit my lower lip in desire as I spoke, “So what did the prof want?”

She shrugged indifference, but her smile gave her away. “She just wanted to submit some of my poems about you for some Boston publication, or some other nonsense like that.”

As I perked up with a giant smile leaning back into her to show my excitement over the announcement, Vicky stood on the bed and started jumping around yelling excitedly. “Oh, my Gawd! How friggin' awesome is that!?”

I was almost giggling as I said, “Baby! That's wonderful!” Then I remembered. “Oh, that reminds me, I almost forgot that Mrs. Sax told me that while I was out of commission I won that silly collegiate art competition. Some crazy person made a forty thousand dollar offer on the piece.”

This was apparently a mistake on my part as I now had two girls jumping on the bed squealing. As we settled and the girls sat back down, Vicky spoke grabbing one of each of our hands, "You two are like, super amazing and talented! Not to mention like the cutest couple... ever!"

I was blushing badly at this point as Valla said, "Damn straight!"

We all sat around and gossiped for an hour or so until the topic of the future came up. I clammed up and Vic noticed, then offered, "Well, ummm... why don't you two talk while I go out to get us some Chinese takeout. I should be gone what? An hour? Two?" She jumped off the bed and started toward the door but was stopped by Valla grabbing her hand.

She looked up at the little blonde and spoke so quietly that it was almost inaudible. "No, stay." Then she continued a little louder, "You have a right to know too. You two are my only friends. My best friends." She kissed my neck gently, sending a shiver through me. "And you... more."

Valla let her hand drop as Vicky just nodded then whipped out her phone, her eyes watering as she dialed the number for the Chinese restaurant from memory (duh). "All you had to do was say 'just order in.'" She forced her customary smile back onto her face and speaking into her phone, "Hi! Yeah, I'm going to need the family combo number twelve delivered to UW Dorm C, room 211. Yup, this is her. Okay. Yeah just on the card. Thanks." She hung up and joined us back on the bed.

Not much was said while we waited for the food, we all silently understood we would wait until after we ate to talk. I reflected on how scarily in sync the three of us were.

So we played cards, but Vicky kept pushing the card box crooked on the nightstand, causing me to keep reaching over to straighten it out. “Slap Jack!” she squealed as I finally realized she was just creating diversions.

No wonder I've never won when I played her. “Hey! Wait a minute you little blonde cheat!” I said as I nudged the box back and forth perfectly into place.

A hot breath on my neck caused goosebumps down my flesh as Valla whispered in a husky, hungry voice, “No, that's okay. It's so hot.” She place a nip on my neck. I'm not too proud to admit that I might have squeaked.

After the food had arrived we sat on the floor eating straight from the cartons. I glanced at the two girls smiling as they watched me meticulously arrange each bite in the carton with my chopsticks before I shoveled them into my mouth. Noodles are the bane of my existence, they are so... random. “Hey, you're making me self-conscious here!” I complained. They both cracked up as I shook my head at them, then grabbed my water bottle to wash the food down.

Vicky cleaned up our mess and Valla turned off the overhead light. The only light in the room came from the little lamp on the nightstand. We dressed in our night clothes and all sat cross-legged on Valla's bed. She looked at Valla and me, "Now. About the future."

The three of us spoke until two in the morning about our secrets, our hopes and dreams and goals in life. Where we wanted to end up, how we envisioned things. We cried over Valla, we laughed with each other, we contemplated heavy subjects that people our age shouldn't be burdened with. We bared our souls to each other. I marveled over how my entire life I have never felt so close to two people and never believed I could ever experience love, especially from someone as amazing as my Valhalla. Now there are two people on the planet that know her true name.

Valla told us of the checklist of four things she had vowed to accomplish before her affliction took her from this world. She made the list when she was very young and being told that a normal life for her was not possible. Even back then, she had refused to be defined by her disease. But the first one on the list she told herself she would accomplish no matter what, for her father's memory. The final three were just what she defined as the yardstick for a successful life.

1. Graduate College
2. Find Love
3. Get Married
4. Have a Child

“I can scratch number two off the list now,” she whispered as she pulled me into her, me laying my head in the crook of her neck.

I whispered back, “I can help with the list.”

Valla's eyes widened at that and Vic smiled at us.

Vicky's list was similar but instead of a child she wanted a successful professional career. For how perky and bubbly she was, underneath it all she was just as insecure and scared as the rest of us.

1. Graduate College
2. Find Love
3. Get Married
4. Successful Career

I could only think of two things I wanted. I know I was being selfish, but really they were the only two things that would not leave the broken loop of my obsessive compulsive thinking. Neither girl judged me.

1. Graduate College
2. Spend Every Available Minute With Valla

Vicky smiled softly when she heard mine. I looked down, chancing quick glances between them. “That's how I want to define myself. This thing I found with her was an impossibility in my life. She IS my miracle.”

After a few minutes of silence, we were all showing signs of exhaustion. Wordlessly Valla and I cuddled into each other, my back to her front, her arm draped across my waist. Vicky looked over at her bed, then back at us with a sad look. I raised my arm, inviting her, and she slid in front of me, my arm draping over her waist.

I whispered to the two sadly, "Tomorrow I lose the crutch and I go back to my dorm. I'm going to feel so isolated."

Vicky mumbled quietly, half asleep, "No, you stay here with us. We can all use your room for a place to get away and be alone whenever we need."

Valla grunted in agreement. I felt a tear roll down my cheek as we all drifted to sleep.

Chapter 11 – Art Final

The weeks flew past, what remained of the semester was going past in a blur. Thanksgiving struck like lightning. Valla and had I planned on having turkey TV dinners in the VV Lair since we both had no family. However our arms were almost pulled out of or sockets when we were dragged to Vicky's parents, along with Molly who was now becoming a regular in the Lair or over at my dorm room with Vicky.

After detouring around the remnants of yesterday's annual iFORk Children's Festival, we made our way to the Davenport's house. Victoria's parents lived in a friggin' mansion. It was kind of amazing that her parents didn't even bat an eye finding out that she was dating a girl and that Valla and I were a couple. They doted on us like we were family. Mrs. Davenport thanked me no less that ten times that night for saving Vicky from the attack and telling me to call her Maira. I could see where the hyperactivity in Vic came from.

The meal was awesome. Probably the best home cooked meal I can ever remember. The atmosphere there just felt like family to me. I told the girls later that I had amended my checklist to include 'family.' They just nodded in approval and I was rewarded with hugs.

The following weeks were punctuated by smiles, laughs and togetherness. Our tight bond was growing at an exponential rate.

Then the end of the semester and Christmas break was approaching at breakneck speeds, just two days of finals to go. I had received the forty thousand dollars from New York and an additional seventy-two thousand dollars from the sale of four pieces from the student gallery auctions the prior week. Vicky helped me set up a savings and investment portfolio for the funds and for future earnings. Segregating a percentage for a tax-deferred retirement fund. Wow is all I can say.

By that time, Valla had her poems published in multiple monthly publications, gaining her sizable commissions of her own. Vicky worked her wizardry there too and reorganized my girl's inheritance as well. Valla was in contact with a publisher that wanted to create a book of her works. I couldn't have been prouder of my girl.

Each of us was sneaking off with Vic's car from time to time, purchasing Christmas gifts or supplies for creating some. I made a mental note to myself that eventually I'd need to get a car of my own. Public transit sucked and I felt bad borrowing Vicky's all the time.

Unknown to the girls, the past three weeks Mrs. Sax and I would sneak off campus for a little over an hour during class for a special project I was commissioned for by the city. My 'final' in her class.

I had only had one episode the past four weeks, I think it freaked Molly out a bit as Vicky and I just continued our game of slapjack through it. She would only meet Vicky over at my dorm room for a week.

The trial for the three that had attacked Vicky and I resulted in just two years of probation for the two that joined Max while he got twelve months in jail and two years probation since he had used a weapon. It seemed pretty lenient to me, but at least they were paying for the crime in some manner.

Things are going well. I thought to myself as I sat, losing yet another game of slapjack to Vicky and Molly on the floor of the Lair. I was busy straightening out the card box to the edge of the throw rug that Molly had "accidentally" bumped... again. When Valla walked in, I looked up and smiled. "Slap Jack!" Molly screamed.

Everyone but me laughed. "Cheaters." I pouted and hissed under my breath. Vic merely shot her infectious smile at me.

"Yet you play every time Mia."

I tried to stop my own smile from appearing, I failed.

Valla sat behind me with her hands on my stomach, her thumbs rubbing random circles on what little-exposed skin was showing. Now that casts were off and we were all healed fully this was torture, I was scared that my arousal was obvious to everyone. She kissed me behind my ear and received the whimper from me that she wanted before she spoke.

"So, I just finished my last final! I'm free! Vickster was done yesterday, that leaves you, my love." She nuzzled me.

I gasped raggedly and said, “I just have to turn in my art final tomorrow and I am all yours for holiday break baby.” I looked back at her with a smile, then over to Vicky, who was busy aggressively marking her territory on Molly's neck. “I need you two to be there with me when I turn it in if that is okay.”

Vicky glanced proudly at her red creation on Molly's neck then looked over at me. “Nervous? Your stuff is amazing Mia. There's nothing to worry about. But we'll be there of course. Oh speaking of being there, what plans you two got over break?”

I shrugged. “I don't have anywhere to go, so I was planning on hanging out here.”

Valla chimed in, “Me too.”

That got us a rare “Bullshit!” from Vicky. “You two are coming home with me!” she said sweetly. Crinkling her eyes and scrunching up her nose with a genuine, patented closed mouth Victoria Smile.

“Jesus that was cute!” Valla laughed, “How can we say no to that?”

I agreed and glanced a question over to Molly.

“Nope,” she said. “I'm flying back to San Francisco in the morning to be with the fam. They aren't too, ummm... open and accepting about Vic and I. So I leave her in your capable hands, but do request that you return her in the same condition as when you received her.”

In unison Valla and I chirped out, “No promises!” Causing laughter all around.

Molly bumped the card box just to be mean. I ignored it... for an entire two seconds then straightened it up.

"Gawd I want you," was hotly whispered into my ear by my love, stopping all brain function instantly. Then the tease stood up and went to the restroom, swinging her hips suggestively.

"Nice Vee!" Vicky giggled and grabbed all the cards, stuffed them in the box, and stood, placing a hand on my shoulder as she passed to put them away. "Mia... don't forget to breathe," she bubbled out in mirth.

I exhaled finally. Molly got up and sat on Vicky's bed while I stood and moved to the desk chair.

When Valla walked back in the room Molly asked if we wanted to hit the Christmas party at the Steam Plant Club tonight. In harmony, three voices snapped, "No!"

Valla chuckled, "I think we've had enough of parties for a while."

Molly stood and did a fake stretch and yawn, eyeballing Vicky and biting her lower lip. "Well, I have to be up at o' too damn early to catch my plane. Drive me to my apartment schoolgirl?"

Vicky smiled and stood to grab her purse. I stood suddenly and exclaimed, "Oh wait, Molly!" I dug in one of the bags of wrapped Christmas presents beside the desk and pulled out a little box and stretched out my hand to Molly. "Merry Christmas from Valla and I!" I said cheerily like a little kid. She smiled and looked at Valla and me, accepted it, then started unwrapping it.

She opened the long white box inside to see the simple, delicate white gold chain inside. She squealed and bent to kiss me on the cheek, then dove on Valla for a hug. “Thank you, Mia, Vee, you shouldn't have.”

I shook my head as I replied, “Yes we should have, you make Victoria happy.”

Vicky started talking as she looped her arm in Molly's and started toward the door. “Be back in an hour...” Molly held two fingers up at her with a seductive smile, “...umm I mean two hours with dinner.” As they left the room I swear I heard Vicky say something to Molly hungrily under her breath that sounded suspicious like, “Let's see just how happy you can make me.”

Valla and I looked at each other, then erupted into laughter. She pulled me to my feet and held me close as we danced to imaginary music. I melted into her as I fell in love with her yet again.

We woke the next morning with a dead blonde weight on top of us snoring still holding the slice of pizza she was eating when she fell asleep as we were talking and eating until the wee hours of the morning. Valla reached over me to grab the pizza slice and placed it on the pizza box on the floor, then she gently pulled Vicky off the top of us and onto the bed between us.

We just sat there in the early morning gazing at each other over the snoring blonde. Her catlike eyes communing with my emerald. I liked lazy mornings like this the best, but it wouldn't last long as my 'art final' wasn't in class after lunch, it was at 9:00 am. I'd have to tell them soon, but I was so comfortable right now.

We each draped an arm over Vicky's shoulder so we could touch each other, sharing our love through the contact. We sat this way smiling for a while and my internal chronometer chimed. “It's eight,” I whispered, and Valla looked behind me at the alarm clock as it clicked over from 7:59 to 8:00.

She smiled and looked back to me and whispered, “So? We don't have anywhere to be until 1:00.”

I looked at her with a guilty look on my face and whispered, “Umm... we have to be somewhere by 9:00 am to turn in my final.”

Her eyes narrowed in confusion. “Why didn't you say anything? Okay, let's get blondie up.”

Vic just stretched like a cat between us. “Mmmm don't bother I'm up. Ooooo I'm the meat in a lesbian sandwich!”

I slapped her shoulder as I sat up. “Perve!”

She blinked at us innocently. “What? You guys are the ones giving me good material for my masturbation sessions!”

I looked at her in shock and Valla just laughed out loud. “Oddly, I don't take offense.”

We began our choreographed dance of stripping bodies, showers were taken, hair brushing, and fresh clothing donned that we had developed over the past few weeks. Though it would seem impossible for three college-aged girls, just a half hour later we were ready for the day.

As we walked out of the dorm building, the girls started to turn right toward the art building and I grabbed their arms and swung them around toward the parking lot. They looked confused and I cut off any questions. “My final is sorta down at the waterfront at Pike Place Market. No questions, just come.”

I got some squishy eyed looks from the other lez-migos, but they didn't ask. “What's she up to?” We joked and laughed our way to the parking garage at the end of the market, then we walked down the stairs to the boardwalk. We walked just past the other end of Pike Place and crossed back over the street under the viaduct, to where a bunch of people were gathered by a tall brick building with a huge tarp draping the entire wall.

We saw Mrs. Sax waving at us and we joined her by her side as she spoke, “This is exciting! They are going to unveil it in just a couple minutes.” She glanced at the confused and lost looking girls with me. “Oh... you haven't told them?” I shook my head. She smiled at them. “You are going to love this!”

I was getting nervous. “J-jenny, this is V-Vicky and Valla.”

Jenny gasped staring at Valla. “Why have I never seen it before? This is her?” she asked as she looked back at the tarp, then turned to me after shaking their hands. I just nodded.

She smiled back at Valla, who said, “Call me Vee.”

There was a feedback screech in the PA system as a man by the wall grabbed a microphone. “Hello everyone, and thanks for coming today. As you know, Seattle has been commissioning urban artwork to beautify our city in recent months. This program has additional goals, such as inspiring other youths to engage in the arts and divert energy into constructive endeavors instead of destructive behavior."

He continued, "It is with my great pleasure that today we'd like to unveil a mural by one of our local students, Miss Mia Jacobs, constructed using thousands of discarded hubcaps that wind up in our landfills each day. I'd like to point out that she miraculously accomplished this feat in less than three weeks."

Then he gestured to the wall and the tarp fell away, there was a collective gasp from the crowd and a few moments of silence, then applauds and whistles erupted from the people gathered.

"Holy shit!" Valla gasped out.

Vicky echoed her shock. "No friggin' way!"

I looked at them to see if it was good or bad shock. They were nothing but smiles, in relief I finally let out the breath I was holding.

I glanced back at the wall to the giant gleaming silver mural of Valla's face smiling into a silver sun. I remember that happy day, it was my inspiration for this mural. I wish all the hubcaps were the same size, I could have done better. If I had more time, I could have taken the...

Mrs. Sax slapped me hard on the arm. "Mia, stop obsessing!" she said sharply, then softened and laughed. "I think you get an A+ on your final."

She turned to Valla and Vicky. "Nice to finally 'officially' meet you, girls. You are all she ever talks about, and I see you at the door with her all the time Vee. But now I have to get back to the University to grade the other finals." She squeezed my arm as the girls nodded acknowledgment, keeping their eyes on the mural as Jenny walked off.

My two friends were both taking pictures with their phones, I was getting uncomfortable. I was grabbing at their arms trying to drag them off. "Valhalla, Victoria! Let's go!" They finally looked away from the mural and to me.

Valla smiled. "Have I ever told you that you are fucking amazing Mia?"

I blushed and nodded. Vic seconded her assessment as we made our way back to the car. Both girls rubbernecking behind us to the mural as we left.

While climbing the stairs, Valla turned to me with amazement twinkling in her eyes as she asked, "When? How?"

I smiled triumphantly then said, "The past three weeks, Jenny and I have been sneaking out of class after you drop me off and coming back before you arrive to pick me up."

Valla smiled and bit her bottom lip then husked out, "I'd take you right here right now on these steps if Vic weren't here!"

That got me so aroused and embarrassed that it was hard to walk. Vicky chimed in, "Don't mind me, I was thinking the same thing after seeing that work of art!" I don't think I had ever blushed so hard as the girls laughed.

Valla's sexual innuendo has been ramping up to almost critical mass the closer we got to Christmas. All I can think about lately because of it is her promise to me from Halloween. And after her comment just now, I'd give myself to her in a moment right here and now if she was serious.

They snapped me out of my happy fantasies as we reached the car, Valla waving her hand in front of my eyes. Vicky started bouncing around in her seat. “So! Let's get back to the Lair and grab our luggage and get the heck over to my folks house! We're finally FREE till after New Years!” she babbled out at speeds faster than light. We started laughing as she cranked the radio and we rocked out back to the dorm.

On a random thought, I added to my loop that I'll have to remind myself later to deposit the thirty-two thousand dollar check I got for the mural commission. Vicky would kill me if I just leave a check lying around the Lair again.

Chapter 12 – Magical Christmas

This Christmas Eve... I don't even have words for it... it was just so amazingly surreal to me. I can mostly remember the excitement of Christmas from before my parents died, but those memories are also colored by the point of view of a child. But this was on a whole new level.

The only decent Christmas after that was the one when I was with the Cohans. They were extremely poor, so we didn't do much, but Christmas morning was great. There were magically two presents under the empty tree for me. They had bought me a new hoodie and some paint brushes. I cried. I gave them the artwork I had made for them that year... a portrait of them when viewed from across the room, created with small colored sticker dots.

But this was something altogether different. The Davenports had apparently conspired with Vicky, who knew we would try to stay in the dorm for the holidays. They brought us on a short drive to just above Issaquah into the Cascades, above the snowline to a charming timber-framed outdoor outfitter's place named Silent Bob's. Geek much? We spent most of the day going through a true winter wonderland in a sleigh pulled by a team of Clydesdales.

I cuddled into Valla under a warm blanket as we watched the snow covered trees, frozen lakes, and mountain peaks pass by. It was so tranquil none of us spoke often, we were just basking in the ambiance and majesty of nature. It was magical.

At lunch time, the sleigh stopped at a campsite covered by a large timber frame picnic area that was decorated with holly wreaths and garlands with big red bows. From hidden speakers somewhere, just barely audible, instrumental Christmas music was being piped in.

At the far end was a huge fireplace constructed of large stones where a roaring fire kept the picnic table area quite cozy despite the cold. There was a beautiful picnic lunch laid out on white lace tablecloths for the five of us, complete with hot cocoa and marshmallows. I felt like I was in an old black and white holiday movie.

Maira watched me poke at Valla's utensils with my finger, straightening them out every time Valla put them down between bites. Valla's eyes never leaving me, her smiling and biting her lower lip each time she put a fork down crooked. Finally, Maira looked at Vicky and spoke under her breath, but I was able to catch it, "What are they doing?"

Vicky wasn't quiet at all, giggling out her response, "Oh, that? Vee is just turning herself on. Mia's OCD makes her hot, it's like watching porn to her."

Now I don't know who was more embarrassed at that point; Valla, Maira, or myself. I wanted to find a place to hide. I buried my head in Valla's shoulder. Mrs. Davenport slapped Vicky's arm admonishing, "Victoria Amelia Davenport!"

Vicky held her hands up in defense saying. “What? It's true!” Maira just shook her head and smiled at her daughter's antics. Mr. Davenport was just laughing at the whole incident.

After lunch, we were loaded back up in the sleigh and returned on a shorter, more direct path to the car. We sang Christmas carols in the car on the way back to the Davenport's place, laughing and having such a great time.

When we got back to the Davenport's it was dark. We settled in the great room that was decked out with white Christmas lights, beautiful natural garlands, and red bows. The stone fireplace burned romantically with big, red, empty stockings, each of our names embroidered on them in gold thread, hanging from the mantle.

But the focus of the room was the large tree in the corner by the huge panoramic windows. The twinkly white lights and the beautiful glass ornaments with red bows tied to the branches, presents tucked neatly under the tree, just felt so... right. The place looked like a fairyland. My eye caught something and I walked over to the tree then looked at an ornament that was not like the others.

It was an unevenly constructed snowflake made from Popsicle sticks covered with glitter, and the picture of an adorable little blonde girl in the middle. The contagious smile on her face was unmistakable, I caught myself smiling back at the photo. It was Victoria, she couldn't have been older than five in the picture. Maira stepped beside me. “Yes, it is my favorite ornament. Vicky made it for me in the first grade.”

I smiled back at her then turned my gaze to Valla, laughing on the couch at something Mr. Davenport had just said. This truly did feel like family, I'm glad that Valla got a chance to experience it with me. Unbidden, my eyes teared up a bit as I watched her. I whispered to Mrs. Davenport, “Thank you so much for everything you are doing for us. This is so wonderful, you truly didn't have to go through all this effort. You have no clue how much this means to us.”

I glanced over at her, she was looking at Valla too, with sorrow in her eyes. I looked at her and Valla and back again I opened my mouth to speak, but she nodded and whispered to me, “We know about Vee.” I knew she was talking about Valla's secret, it was like there was a vise on my heart. How did they know?

“V-Vicky?” I asked.

She shook her head slowly and turned her sad eyes back to me. “No. She'd never betray you girls' trust. It's just obvious.”

I nodded and silently cried. She stepped between Valla and me so she wouldn't see. She reached up and wiped away my tears with her sleeve, then grabbed my hand and dragged me to the giant sectional couch beside my girl before she spoke, “Let's watch a holiday movie before we have our Christmas feast, shall we everyone?” Everyone cheerfully piped up in agreement as Mr. Davenport grabbed the remote and turned on the flat screen TV and cued up Santa Clause is Coming to Town.

About when we were all singing, “You put one foot in front of the other, and soon you'll be walkin' 'cross the flo-o-or!” Mrs. D excused herself to check on dinner. I was cuddled into the crook of Valla's arm while Vicky was laying across our laps with her head in my lap and her feet draped across her father. It was nice. I gave Valla a gentle peck on the lips as she lazily ran her fingers through Victoria's hair as we watched the show.

Just as the show was finishing, Maira came in with a smile. “Dinner is ready everyone!” We got up excitedly following the heavenly smells wafting from the dining room. Vicky hopped up on my back and I gave her a piggyback ride in while Valla and Mr. D laughed at our antics.

Mr. Davenport sat at the head of the table while his wife took the other end. We three girls sat along one side, with Vic close to her mother. Mr. D spoke, “We're going to forgo saying grace this year and instead just give thanks for the wonderful family we have here and that we can share of ourselves at this time.”

Everyone smiled in agreement. “Here here,” we chimed and started dishing up. There was lots of chatting, gossip, and laughing going on throughout the meal. The food was perfect and the ham was delicious. More than a few times I had to straighten Valla's utensils, the vixen.

Throughout the meal, I would sit back and marvel at 'family'. Valla never looked happier. I decided then and there that I was going to make sure Valla had her entire list checked off, one way or another.

After helping clean up after the meal, we all retired down the hall to the bedrooms. Valla and I were in the guestroom that shared an adjoining bathroom with Vicky's room. We dressed in our night clothes, I kissed Little Vee good night and put her in my purse.

We were exhausted and happy as we started to doze off in each others arm. Sometime during the night, Victoria wandered in hugging a pillow to her chest. "I miss Molly," she whispered, and we wordlessly raised the covers for her to slide in with us.

We woke up to a hyper-blonde pogo-stick bouncing on the bed. "Wake up, wake up, wake up! It's Christmas!"

Valla was giggling at her, "Settle down blondie!" But her excitement was as contagious as her smile. We took turns showering and brushing our teeth but opted to stay in our night clothes.

Vicky grabbed our hands and dragged us to the end of the hall where she called out, "Can we come in?"

Mr. D answered, "Come on in ladies." We rushed in behind Vicky and she pushed us down on the couch beside Mr. and Mrs. Davenport.

Maira smirked and nodded at the little dynamo and Vic rushed over to the fireplace and started grabbing the now overflowing stockings and delivering them to the proper recipients.

Once they were passed out, Vicky hopped up onto the couch beside us like a little kid and we started going through them. Mine had all kinds of candies and fudge wrapped in bright cellophane and a lovely scarf that would go with just about anything. Then there was an assortment of high-quality camel hair paintbrushes that reminded me of that year with the Cohans. I cried again at the memory and thanked the Davenports.

Valla and Vicky were similarly happy about their booty. I was especially impressed with the antique retractable, self-inking fountain pen that Valla got. Then Vicky looked around, seeing everyone had finished, then bounded off the couch and started handing out the presents from under the tree. We must have had at least ten each. I was feeling bad that I only brought each person one gift!

We followed Vicky's lead and started tearing into the presents, or carefully unwrapping and folding the wrapping paper in my case. I was amazed at the beautiful clothing I got as well as the high-end art equipment I had been eyeballing for months. I tried not to cry when I opened my very own easel. Tried is the operative word.

Valla got some stunning clothing as well that I'd love to see on her... or off her. And an amazing calligraphy set with some beautiful huge leather bound books that had only blank pages for her poetry. I saw her tearing up as well.

Vicky got almost exclusively clothing and the most beautiful and delicate sapphire encrusted silver bracelet. It was breathtaking!

Vicky opened the gift from Valla and I and started crying when she saw it. It was a framed photo of the three of us staring off into the night sky. It was her favorite photo of us that was taken by Valla's English Lit professor at an outdoor poetry reading of Valla's works under the stars.

We had pretended to lose it a few weeks ago to get it professionally mounted and matted in a shadowbox frame, with movie ticket stubs from shows we all saw together and a friendship bracelet Valla and I had weaved for her on display.

We were hit by a flying, tackling hug from the pint-sized blonde. We laughed and hugged her back. Then Valla and I each opened our gifts from her. They were matching white gold hearts on whisper thin white gold chains. Mine was inscribed with a script V while Valla's had a script M. We put them on then hugged Vicky ourselves, they were so perfect. I couldn't stop smiling.

We turned to Vicky's parents as they opened Valla's gift to them. It was a framed poem done in Valla's calligraphy entitled "Counting". It became my second favorite poem of hers immediately when I spotted the line about a deafening whisper. Maira opened her arms toward Valla. "It's simply moving Vee!" she said as she hugged her, then Mr. D pulled her into a hug too.

Then Maira picked up the larger present from me and removed the wrapping. They were stunned at what looked like a framed black and white portrait of Victoria with her infectious smile. They both leaned in closer to see that it wasn't a photograph, but hundreds of thousands of tiny ink dots that I put on the canvas using a pin I dipped in India ink. I could probably have done better, but I didn't have much time to complete it and... Crap, I'm obsessing again!

It was Maira's turn to cry as I got the same hug treatment from the two of them that they had just given Valla. Then I turned to Valla and pointed to the present from me to her. She had been looking at it all morning, hovering around it, revering it but keeping her distance. She finally removed the wrapping paper and opened the box. She looked in and her jaw dropped, she looked closer. “Are those words? They are. They say... Oh, my god! Mia!”

She pulled the sculpted three-dimensional white heart that resembled a delicate wire frame made of paper ribbons that I had actually carved out of a single piece of wood. I used a red hot sewing needle to burn thousands of tiny holes through the wood ribbons to form the words from her poem 'Every Day' into it. She was openly crying and smiling now. I finally exhaled, relieved that she liked it.

I went to hug her but got a knee buckling passionate kiss instead. She had to support me to prevent my collapse. I wasn't complaining as I did the only thing a sane person would do when the sexiest person alive was kissing them... I returned the kiss, my entire being was buzzing.

After I came back down to Earth, I started cleaning up the discarded wrapping paper from the floor around everyone. I couldn't handle it strewn about haphazardly anymore though I had tried to ignore it, I needed to fold them neatly and throw them away. But Valla grabbed my hand saying, "No, not yet. There's still one more." She made me sit back down on the couch.

She nervously brought her other arm from behind her back, displaying a small wrapped box and handed it to me. I happily started meticulously removing the little ribbon and wrapping paper as she spoke, "Mia. Life is too short. I wish I could promise you forever. But all I can promise is to give you every moment I have. I know it is unfair to ask, but my time is short. I want nothing more than to make you feel loved."

It was a small purple velvet box. I held it up in front of me with reverence, brushing my thumbs across its lid. I steeled myself and flipped the lid open to see the most simple and beautiful, plain white gold band engraved with what looked like Celtic knots. But I could see it was actually a series of Vs and Ms interlaced around it. My jaw dropped as I looked at her, her eyes recapturing mine. I could feel mine starting to water.

She continued with nothing but love sparkling away in her amazing eyes, "Mia Jessica Jacobs... will you make me the happiest woman alive and marry me?"

Before her last syllable was out, I replied, "YES! ...I could live a lifetime in your eyes." Her lips were on mine, I had never felt such a soulful kiss from her. I poured my heart into hers as we breathed each other's breath.

She broke the kiss and pulled back gasping, then pulling the ring from its cushion she slid it onto my finger. Tears of happiness were flowing unchecked down both our cheeks. I brought my fingers to my lips, reliving that kiss. I turned to the Davenports to see the two ladies hugging, smiling and crying while watching us.

Mr. Davenport cleared his throat in typical male fashion, pretending to not be misting up and hoarsely said, “This calls for a celebration! Hot cocoa and a movie?” We all laughed and settled in on the couch as Mrs. D hurried off and brought in mugs of hot chocolate and cookies a couple short minutes later.

As the movie, Breakfast at Tiffany's rolled the ending credits Valla spoke to the group, “Would it be okay if I stole this enchanting pixie for a few hours? I know it is Christmas day, but there's something I have to show her. If there aren't any other plans.” We were assured that nothing pressing was lined up. With a promise of being back in plenty of time for dinner, we got dressed and borrowed Vicky's car keys then set off down the road.

Chapter 13 – Homecoming

As we drove, Valla put some music on the radio and we rocked out, bobbing and singing and laughing. I got distracted many times by the shiny ring glistening on my finger. Valla had to poke me several times to knock me out of my happy fog as I stared at it. "Earth to Mia!" She giggled as I snapped out of it again offering her a huge toothy smile, wiggling my fingers at her showing off the ring.

"What? It ain't often I can show proof to the world that the perfect woman chose me!" I flirted back, but sincerely meaning my words.

She bit her lip seductively and I melted. Damn her and the power she has over me! I grabbed her right hand as she drove and laced our fingers. "So, you still haven't told me where we are going." I probed, not making it a question.

"Home," she said with a mischievous grin. That's all she offered me as we sat in a comfortable silence the rest of the drive. Just soaking in each others presence.

We crossed Lake Washington at Evergreen Point and wound up at Yarrow Bay. She pulled into the driveway of a beautiful waterfront summer home and parked in front of the door. We got out and I looked around. The house itself was single level construction with a whimsical, storybook feel. All creams and browns with a bright green, inviting door. The attached three car garage was huge with a matching green door. It was clear it was an expansive home in the back, but charmingly subtle in the front.

Valla jumped out of the car with a smile and ran around to open my door and help me out. How friggin' sweet is she? Then I started noticing some things about the house and property. The yard was unkempt and overgrown in areas that looked to have been gorgeous landscaping at one point. The windows were water spotted and muddy dust caked a lot of the horizontal surfaces from lack of maintenance.

She still hadn't said a word and I didn't want to be the first to vocalize. I could tell by her movements that this is something she needed to do, it was important to her. The front door deadbolt had an electronic keypad and she punched in a four digit code and twisted the lock. It thunked open and she pushed it in, gesturing for me to enter with a dazzling smile and a twinkle of mischief in her catlike eyes.

I walked in and looked around. The large open living room went the entire depth of the home, with huge glass panels in the back wall revealing a large yard with a dock stretching out to the lake. The furniture and hanging lamps were all covered in white sheets with dust covering the sheets. The polished stone floor was inlaid with walnut to form a lattice pattern on the floor and the giant area rug under the sitting area was dull with dust.

Even in its unused state it was breathtaking. I turned to see Valla smiling like the Cheshire Cat. “Home.” She grabbed my hand

and interlaced our fingers. She leaned in and gave me a barely there kiss, our lips shared a whisper of contact. She didn't move away. Instead she just smiled and spoke, her lips nicking mine as she did, "I figured that we'd need a place of our own if you had said yes to me."

I blinked. "Of course I was going to say yes! I said yes long before you asked today. How could you have thought otherwise?"

She gave me another quick kiss and backed off still holding my hand as she spoke softer, "This was my home growing up. Until... my father died two years ago from a brain tumor. I haven't been back here since."

Her face saddened and she looked far away as she spoke of him. I had never pushed her on the subject of her father. "My whole life I knew I would be gone before him. It was supposed to be a fact. But it goes to show you that nothing in life is certain. He was my best friend. It was just a matter of three months between when they found the tumor and when he left me."

I gave her hand a gentle squeeze. She continued, "I applied to be an emancipated minor instead of getting lost in the social services machine. I had to get out of here, too many memories to haunt me. I rented an apartment with funds from my inheritance and finished my senior year in high school. I got the scholarship in English literature that we had both dreamed of for me. We had the money to put me through the college of my choice, but I wanted to do it all on my own merit."

She turned to me and her wistful, melancholy expression turned into something softer and tinged with want. “And I found the love of my life.” Her voice was huskier. She bit her lower lip, melting me to the core. “With you, we can make this feel like a home again... If you want.” She looked, searching for an answer to her question in my eyes.

I smiled back, entranced by her ever-changing eyes. “It's beautiful. I love it. And to be totally, honest, home for me is YOU... Wherever you are. I'm so in love with you Valhalla Abbey Taylor.” She looked both relieved and happy all at once.

She licked her lips, her eyes darkened with lust. I could feel it radiating off of her in waves, causing interesting things to happen to some embarrassing areas on my anatomy. God, I want her! She turned and pulled me behind her as she went down a hall, to the right, and past what looked like a master bedroom into a smaller one.

With one hand she ripped the white sheet off the bed, causing a small dust cloud, and then she pushed me backward onto the bed with her straddling me. Her voice was husky and raspy with desire. “I gave you a promise. It's time.” My entire body became a tingling inferno as I remembered her promise. My toes curled when her lips crushed against mine, her hands desperately clawing off my clothes. Although I despise the word, as it seems so crude and raw, I had never felt so horny in my life.

Now let me tell you even though neither of us had any experience with lesbian sex and felt we didn't know what to do, our bodies were so in sync that we instinctively knew what to do to please each other. Valla's face had never looked as beautiful as when she was climaxing. It was a new goal in my life to see that expression as often as possible. And the amazing things she did to me I didn't think were possible!

So anyway, needless to say, she fulfilled her promise to me... twice... and with interest! If it were possible to die from over-arousal, I'm sure I was on the cusp of it. As we laid in each others arms, sweat soaked hair across our faces and basking in the afterglow I raggedly offered, “You know, I think I might be gay.” We both laughed hard and kept laughing every time we looked at each other.

My sides were hurting so bad by the time we could look at each other without cracking up. But then our eyes locked, amber meeting emerald and I felt my lust resurfacing.

Valla was stronger than me. “We will never leave this bed if we don't get up now. Let's get cleaned up and I'll give you the tour.”

I growled, “I'll clean you up... again.” Licking my lips and staring at her crotch seductively, my mouth watering. She stood and pulled me to my feet, placing a quick but passionate kiss on my lips. God, she tastes great.

With a playful laugh she whispered, “I've created a monster.” Then she shooed me into the attached bathroom. “Should be towels in the cupboard, soap and shampoo under the sink.”

I started the shower grumbling in my frustrated state. Then smiled to myself knowing that I was hers as I washed away our earlier activities.

Once I was cleaned up, I realized there wasn't a blow dryer there so I dried my hair the best I could, running my brush through the long tresses of ebony. Valla wandered back into the room with a towel around her. I assumed she used another bathroom in the house. I would have welcomed her into the shower with me, but this was smarter. We would have wound up on the floor of the shower an hour later and still panting if she had.

She sat me on the bed and grabbed the brush from me, running her fingers through my hair to fluff it up and get air circulating through it to dry faster as she brushed. Is it wrong that I found that hawt too? Did she just smell my neck? When she was satisfied, she gave me a quick kiss on my pulse point, sending goosebumps across my flesh. Then she whispered, “God, I love your long raven hair.”

Then I returned the favor and worked on her hair. Her brown locks were so luxurious feeling as they slid between my fingers. I could do this all day. I enjoyed pampering her. She moaned in satisfaction, “That feels good baby. Have I mentioned how much I love you, Mia?” I kissed her behind the ear in answer as I finished up the best I could with her hair.

We dressed quickly and she proceeded to drag me out of her childhood bedroom and around the house for a whirlwind tour. She showed me the guest room then the huge master suite with a walk-in closet that was bigger than the VV Lair, and the huge master bathroom with two showers and a giant jetted tub on a pedestal in the middle.

The kitchen was unbelievable with a white marble tile floor, a breakfast bar on the food prep island, and the black walnut cabinets accentuated with stainless steel hardware that matched all of the stainless steel appliances and exhaust hood. The black granite counters were a counterpoint to the floor.

The dining area was just an extension of the kitchen area. It gave a warm, friendly feel to an otherwise huge space. It flowed out to the living space I had seen earlier. I noticed the large stone fireplace dominating a wall by the seating area in the great room. Someone had put a lot of thought into the layout of this house. We were talking about anything and everything, often breaking into fits of laughter.

Then she dragged me out to the kitchen again and through a side door to the attached garage. It was huge, with a polished concrete floor. Workbenches along one wall were covered with sheets and on the far end was a large vehicle covered like everything else. “We could set up a studio for you in here,” she whispered in my ear, her breath hot on my neck.

Last stop was back into the living room and then outside through one of the huge glass panels I thought was a window but was actually a swiveling door on seemingly invisible hinges. She laced our fingers as we walked along a winding cobblestone path to the dock. We bundled into our coats from the bitter winter wind and sat on the end of the dock, swinging our feet in the air as children, to continue our chat.

"So? Whaddaya think? Can you see us living here?" She looked hopeful.

I alleviated any doubt with my response, "It couldn't be more perfect... just like you." We kissed for a few moments, not the animalistic kissing from earlier, but tender, gentle kisses meant only to convey our love.

We looked out over the lake, watching a small plane with purple wingtips and a big wavy purple stripe on it lazily flying above the water, and we shivered. "Brrr," she stated with a silly grin, kicking away with her combat boot encased feet.

"Yeah, brrr." I smiled back. We got up and made our way back inside, she made a quick detour to the garage to grab a garage door opener from a hook on the wall and put it in her purse.

"Ready hot stuff?" she asked, wiggling her eyebrows.

"Always!" I replied happily as we walked out the front door.

We took a step after she locked the door before she stopped and pulled me back by our intertwined hands. "Just a sec," she said with a smile as she pressed a few buttons on the lock "There... now type in a four digit code." I typed my debit card pin number and the number pad flashed a couple of times.

She then pulled me along to the car almost skipping, speaking back to me, "Now you can get into OUR house anytime!"

I said, "Our... our... I like how that tastes on the tongue."

Valla rolled her eyes. "You're a weird one Mia Jacobs."

I faked offense and voiced, "But I'm yours."

She grinned as she opened the car door for me. "Yes. Yes, you are."

The ride back to the Davenport's home was full of suggestive talk and sexual innuendo. I guess Valla really did create a monster. That's not a bad thing is it? I smiled to myself. We arrived at their house and knocked on the door. Vicky came bounding to the door and swung it open for us.

"Finally! I was going to send out a search party, or like you know, the US Marshals or something. Oh! I'd make an awesome Marshal! How friggin' amazing would that be? I..." She paused before we could tell her to slow down to human speeds then her eyes went wide and she almost screamed, "OMG! You totally did it! Was it as awesome as I imagined? Like did you break the bed or anything?"

In unison Valla, Maira (who had just walked up), and I shouted, "Vicky!" I was trying to find a hole to hide in as Valla dragged me past her toward the couch.

I caught her whisper at Vic as we passed, “We did, it was, and almost.” She was smirking as Vicky lit up like the Christmas tree. I'm sure I eeped, but all I could hear was the blood rushing through my ears. Maira was just shaking her head at everyone's antics.

The next few days at the Davenport's were punctuated with steamy love making sessions every chance we could sneak away. I was beginning to see a direct correlation between my smile and my zipper. And even when others were around Valla kept me on the top end of the arousal scale by sneaking passing touches and stealing kisses. I think she was taking it as her sacred duty to see if she couldn't make that my natural state of being around her. Not that I was complaining... at all... in any way.

New years Eve came around and Vicky was standing in a corner holding her phone, looking sad and wasn't her usual ball of energy. I pulled her aside. “What's up blondie?”

She looked at me with puppy-dog eyes. “Molly isn't coming back.”

I was shocked. “What? Why?”

Her eyes flared with anger for a moment then settled back into sadness. “Her parents believe I'm a bad influence on her and 'tricked' her into thinking she liked girls now. She doesn't want to 'disappoint' them anymore, so she is moving back with them down there. She says I could be her 'secret' and we could do a long distance thing.” She looked at me half broken. “Is that what I am? A disappointment and a secret?”

I pulled her into a hug and she buried her head in my shoulder and cried silently. I motioned Valla over with my eyes. She hurried over and led us, still hugging, into Vicky's room as I tried to calm her. "Shh... shhh Victoria. You are not now, nor could you ever be a disappointment! And nobody, I mean NOBODY has the right to hide you away and make you their dirty little secret! You are an amazing girl and if anyone puts anything above that they never deserved to have you! Got it?"

She sniffled a little, then looked up into our three-way hug. "I love you guys, you know that? I don't know why I deserve such amazing friends."

Valla shook her head at that and whispered, "We love you too Vicky. Cause YOU are amazing. Us three lez-migos gotta stick together!"

This finally got a grin from her as she looked between us. "Oooo I'm the meat again!" We all shared a laugh and sat there for a minute for her to compose herself before making our way back out to the couch.

Minutes later our extended family and we were chanting, "5-4-3-2-1 Happy New Year!" Hugs and kisses were passed around... then a sense of melancholy settled in on us over the fact that it was back to the dorms tomorrow. I was going to miss the feeling of family here.

Chapter 14 – My Valentine

The weeks flew by we were so busy with classwork, art, poem submissions and commissions, cleaning the house to prepare to inhabit, releasing my dorm room back into general population, and getting ready for our wedding. Valla was writing in her leather-bound books between everything else. Knowing time was not on our side we chose Valentine's Day as the date. It was after all a day for love. And gawd did I love Valla!

We gave silent thanks that Washington state is one of the few in the nation (so far) that allows same-sex marriages, since we didn't want to travel for the ceremony. We both asked Vicky to be our maid of honor to which we received a bubbly, “I will soooo make an awesome maid of honor!”

The art community was starting to call my style of remote viewing art the 'Jacob's Effect,' much to my embarrassment and Valla and Vicky's elation.

Vicky was busy too. She was coming out of her post-Molly funk and was starting to dip her toes into the dating pool again. Though it was obvious, she couldn't decide which sex she desired this month. She called it her “taste-testing” phase. Oxford was courting her, and she had added yet another class to her schedule. But there was a dark cloud hanging over her, and I had an inkling as to what it might be.

Conspiring with my partner in crime, life, and the heart, we cornered her one night. Valla offhandedly said, “Boy, I can't believe that we're going to be married in two days Mia.”

I chimed in, “Yeah. It's going to be like the end of an era. It'll be weird moving into our house and not having Vicky around anymore.”

Vicky was getting fidgety and Valla continued, “Yeah, I bet it'll be weird and quiet around here at the Lair without us huh Vic?”

Vicky looked like she was going to cry, and internally I knew Valla was fighting off a smile like I was when Vicky spoke, “Gawd guys. You're gonna make me cry! It is going to be so lonely here without you. And what if they stick me with like a loser roommate? I know I'll see you around campus and junk. We'll still go out and do stuff, but it won't be the same.”

My voice wavered slightly trying to fight a laugh. “Yeah, it's too bad you didn't want to come live with us in our guest room. It woulda' been hella fun, but... oh well.”

Valla added, “Yeah, too bad.”

You could see the gears turning in Vicky's head as she realized what we were doing. “OMG! Really guys? I would so make an awesome housemate! It will be friggin' amazing! I could like do the laundry and stuff, and I could...”

Valla and I shouted in unison, “Vicky! Breathe!”

She grabbed me and spun me around twice but just hugged Valla because she couldn't pick her up. I unwound myself twice in the other direction to Valla's lip biting delight, as they hugged. After sharing a laugh, the blonde looked at us in mock anger. “You two know I love you, but I hate you for that! You're mean!” Then she stuck out her tongue to our chuckling.

The next day was spent moving in, leaving just enough stuff at the Lair for our last day. Valla asked me where the rest of my stuff was stored after I had brought over my four boxes, a suitcase of clothing, and my easel. She said we could put it in the garage until we figured out where to put it all in the house.

When I told her that was everything I owned in life, both her and Vicky got a little sad for a moment. When I asked about it, they just said they forgot I was in the foster system most of my life. I was confused, what did that have to do with my stuff? Everyone knows you only keep as much as can fit in the trunk of a car.

The next morning I woke up where I had dozed off, laying on the bed with my head in Valla's lap where she was sitting at the head of the bed on the pillows. Vicky was still on the ground at an awkward angle with her feet up on the bed, the textbook she was speed scanning into her memory last night covering her face as she snored. Sheesh, just how pathetic are we?

The day took forever, I just thought I was counting wrong, but the damn clocks kept agreeing with my count. Finally, after my last class we all rushed off to the VV Lair and grabbed our small bags containing the remainder of our stuff and took one last nostalgic look around this now iconic place in our hearts. We left the keys on the desk and headed off to the Davenport's for what Maira was calling our bachelorette party. And our last sleepover as single women. I like the sound of that!

It was a night full of fun, laughing, crying, talking, and bonding. One of those times you lock away and always treasure.

Morning came and we woke to a hyperactive blondie bouncing on our bed in the Davenport's guest room. “Wake up, wake up, wake up! It's wedding day!” God help me, but I was as excited as her. Valla was groaning and pulling the covers over her head. I joined Vicky in her jumping.

“Wake up, wake up, wake up! It's wedding day!”

Valla dropped the covers from her face, which now had a silly grin plastered across it. “My God! There's two of them!” Then she yelled, “Maira help me!”

A minute later Mrs. D walked in wiping her hands on a dishrag, watching us bouncing on the bed around Valla chanting. “Wake up, wake up!”

She laughed. “Sorry Vee, I'm with the girls on this one.” She yanked the covers off of Valla. Raising her hands in defeat my girl flashed us all a huge smile. “It's wedding day!” I saw Mr. D. walk past the door shaking his head in bemusement at us four squealing women.

Being Friday, we took the day off from our classes for the wedding. We'd be spending our two-day honeymoon in Leavenworth, a scenic Bavarian village two hours from Seattle nestled in the spectacular peaks of the Cascade mountains. I didn't care if we stayed in a burlap sack, I just wanted Valla!

Maira gave us girls a motherly, prideful look. “You ladies need to be getting ready. You are due at the alter in three hours.” She grabbed our hands and gave a squeeze before she let them drop, and she walked out of the room.

While Vicky helped us get dressed, Valla and I spent more time touching each other and making out than paying attention, so Vic called for reinforcements. We were pried apart from each other's lips by Maira and Vicky and forced to dress in separate rooms. My lips missed hers.

“Are you nervous?” Mrs. D. asked as she started fussing with my hair.

I thought about it and smiled. “Actually, I have never felt so sure of anything in my entire life. I just know I can make her happy, and I know that she definitely makes me happy. I still can't believe that she chose... me.”

Maira smiled warmly, then ducked into the adjoining bathroom for a second and came out with various devices and hair care products. She plugged in a curling iron and spoke softly, “I can't believe how good you two are for each other. It is hard to keep a smile off my face when I see you together. You are so genuine with each other. And I have never seen Vicky so happy as when she is around you two. I thank you for that.”

The light went off on the iron and she started putting my long raven hair into tight ringlets. I was curious, I had never curled my hair before since I hid it under my hoodie, it would be interesting to see the outcome. I wish there was a mirror in here.

After a while of curling and teasing, she draped my V necklace on me, which hung perfectly near the cleavage that the white dress exposed. Then she started applying makeup on me. “We're just going to do some light makeup, you are already a natural beauty. Let's see if we can't make your bride growl, shall we Mia?” She laughed at my profuse blushing.

“O-o-okay.”

We had just finished when Vicky came walking in and glanced at me. “Holy shit!” her mouth was hanging open.

Maira snapped, “Language Victoria!”

But Vicky wasn't listening, she looked at me with hungry eyes, taking in the new look her mother gave me as I stood from the bed. “I-is it o-okay?”

Vicky shook her head to snap herself out of it. “Damn girl. It's a good thing you are taken or I wouldn't be responsible for my actions here. You look simply beautiful Mia!” She snapped a picture with her phone, “I'll need that for when I'm alone later.” She waggled her eyebrows as her mother slapped her arm. I blushed profusely as she continued, “Anyway, your blushing bride is waiting. We should really get over to your house for the ceremony. Wouldn't want to be late for your own wedding!”

She turned to leave but turned back to glance at me again. "Wow," she whispered as she walked out of the room. Maira stopped at the door when she noticed I wasn't following. I looked at her nervously then I turned to the attached bathroom to look in the full-length mirror on the door and gasped.

The new looping curls in my hair formed a gently flowing mane around my shoulders that framed my face nicely. The tastefully applied makeup accentuated my eyes and lips enticingly. I looked both innocent and seductive at the same time. I had to look twice. Is this really me?

I smiled at myself in the mirror then over at Mrs. Davenport, and glided out of the restroom on the delicate white stiletto heels I chose so I that could be closer to Valla's lips at the ceremony. Maira led me down the hall and cleared her throat as we approached the great room. I feel pretty.

Valla turned around and both of our breaths hitched. I know I forgot how to breath and my heart forgot how to beat. There, in a matching white dress, was a goddess, no other word would do. Her brown hair almost glowed with its chestnut highlights. Her makeup was perfect. I bit my lower lip in want at her shimmering lips. And the smoky shadow around her eyes made the oranges pop from her light brown pools. Her delicate M necklace drew my attention to her cleavage before my eyes snapped back to hers, getting lost in her sparkling gaze.

She filled out the dress in all the right places and looked to be born of grace and elegance. The best part, for me at least, was the counterpoint... the signature so uniquely Valhalla that it actually worked with this angelic look. Adorning her feet were the combat boots I had grown to love.

I'm pretty sure I was drooling when I finally gained enough cognitive facilities to speak. I somehow remembered that I might need to breath again and finally exhaled before taking another deep breath. Full sentences were still beyond my diminished brain capacity so I uttered the first syllable I could muster, “Hey.”

She blinked a couple times, then bit her lower lip, melting me, and responded in a hoarse, deep voice. “Fucking amazing!” She smiled with a primal hunger and passion I hadn't seen from her before this. She glanced an apology to Maira, who had just about admonished her on her language. Valla licked her lips, “Mia, you look beautiful... no, that word isn't enough. Your hair... you... I.. you're... my God, I just fell in love with you all over again!”

I was so embarrassed now, my blush burning my cheeks but at the same instant I was basking in her adoration and felt oddly proud I could exact this type of reaction from her. I noticed lots of flashes as the Davenports snapped away at us with their cameras and cell phones.

We just stood there drinking in every inch of each other when Vicky stepped between us, clearing her throat, snapping us back to reality. “As much fun as it would be to watch you two have eye sex with each other all day, we have a wedding to get to.”

Mr. D. spoke up, “Vicky, remember... brain/mouth filter.” Then he turned to us. “Ladies, your chariot awaits.” We all filed out the door and into the cars, Valla and I went with Vicky in her Range Rover and the Davenports took their hybrid.

Besides the radio booming Vicky's girl band pop music the ride was silent, with Valla's and my eyes locked in hunger, mentally undressing each other. I must have licked my lips every few seconds.

Vic had to physically remove us one at a time from her car. “You two horndogs can have at each other soon, you gotta go say your I do's first!” She marched us up to the front door as the Davenports joined us and she typed in Valla's code. We never really bothered giving her a code of her own since she had barely glanced when Valla had opened the door once, now the code is burned into her eidetic memory banks.

In just an hour we would be bound together in life as we are in love, I can't wait! We walked through the great room to look at the back yard. The white arbor on the dock decked out in white flowers and sat in front of the five white chairs. There would have been seven but the Cohan's called earlier to let us know they couldn't make it, there was trouble with a foster child. A red carpet runner stretched from the back door to the arbor.

The doorbell rang and Vicky skipped over to get it. The minister walked into the room with her a moment later. He nodded to us with a smile and was intercepted by Vic's parents and dragged outside toward the arbor. The Davenports were nothing if not efficient.

The caterer arrived next with the reception meal for our small gathering, and Vicky had them set up in the great room. Last minute prep was keeping us on our toes, so I was only allowed fleeting glances at my girl. Leaving me biting my lower lip frequently, imagining her on our wedding bed without that dress.

The guests had arrived, and by guests, I mean all two of them. Jenny was first to show, gushing over how Valla and I looked before being led out to the seats by Vic. The second guest, whom we expected because she had, to our shock, requested to be here was last to show up.

Vicky led Missy Hannigan into the room. She stopped short when she saw us with a small smile fighting at the edge of her lips before she stiffened it back to her normal sneer as she greeted Valla. “Freak.”

Valla cordially replied, “Skank.”

Then Missy turned to me. “Spaz.”

I gave her a tiny wave and smile. “Bitch.”

When she asked to come we had inquired as to why, and her terse response led us to believe that she felt responsible for me in some way after the attack. She looked through the back window to see the setup by the dock and just started walking out pausing at the glass panel door with her back to us and said softly away from us, “You two look nice.” She wandered out to take a seat beside Jenny.

A few minutes later Vicky mouthed to us, “It's time.” The butterflies kicked in with a vengeance. This is real. I'm going to be her's! Vicky offered her elbows and each of us accepted one as she led us down the aisle, the violin music playing from the speakers in the arbor.

We reached the minister and Vicky slipped away to her seat beside Frank and Maira as Valla and I turned to each other, our eyes locked with an almost electric current. As one we each bit our lower lips as the music stopped.

Now, you would think that at a defining moment in your lifetime you would pay close attention to what the minister was saying. But if you happen to be standing there looking across at a heavenly creature with longing in her sparkling eyes, then not so much. I mean, I know the guy was talking, but all I could hear was Valla breathing and my own heart beating.

Instinctively I knew an important part was coming up and tuned in a bit. “Do you, Valhalla Abbey Taylor, take this woman to be your lawfully wedded wife?”

Then she was grabbing my hand, causing a white hot fire inside me and slipped the ring the minister had offered onto my finger. Then I experienced that deafening whisper rolling off her glossy lips. “I do. Be my Valentine Mia.” Soft as a breeze.

He then turned to address me, "Do you, Mia Jessica Jacobs, take this woman to be your lawfully wedded wife?"

I blindly took the matching ring he offered me and took her hand in mine. I marveled at its warmth and softness, and graceful fingers with their perfectly manicured nails, then slid the ring on whispering, "I do. Be my Valentine Valla."

Our lips met instantly, it was almost erotic how our lipstick slid and melded together, sticking and dragging as we moved our lips. That was always my favorite part. I tried to send all my love through our contact and could feel hers in return.

I realized the minister was still speaking, "Errrr... well, I now pronounce you wife and wife. You may kiss the brides?" He shrugged and backed off, aware we weren't paying any attention to him.

Mr. Davenport cleared his throat a minute or so later and we reluctantly broke our kiss, gasping and giggling at each other as we looked sheepishly to the spectators.

Vicky was mouthing, "Hawt! Hawt! Hawt!" Everyone else had happy tears in their eyes, Mr. D trying to play it off.

Valla put her cheek next to mine and whispered conspiratorially into my ear, "I'm your wife, Mrs. Jacobs."

I radiated love from my being toward her like a heatwave from within as I whispered back, "And I'm your wife, Mrs. Jacobs."

She grabbed my hand, laced our fingers, and started dragging me back along the red carpet blurting out, "Come on people! Let's get this reception started so I can get my wife to myself!" Everyone cheered at this and followed us inside. Valla coughed.

Lots of hugging and kissing, smiles, and happy tears were involved at the reception, including a super awkward hug for Valla and I from Missy before she left with the customary exchanged insults. I was tapping my foot through the entire reception, just trying to devour Valla with my eyes and our stolen touches and glances. I want her out of that dress, NOW!

Finally, Vicky announced that it was time to release us into the wild so we could go rut like filthy wildebeests. After reminding Vicky about the difference between internal and external dialogue I grabbed Valla's arm and started desperately dragging her to the front door, but she changed our direction and brought us through the kitchen to the garage instead.

I was stunned. The once covered vehicle was sitting there sparkling clean with its gleaming yellow paint. I think it was called an FJ Cruiser or something, I'm not good with car names. The windows had white paint all over them saying "Just married! Now clear a damn path to the hotel!" With little hearts all over. When did Valla get the chance to pull this off? We are usually joined at the hips or lips.

I had thought this whole time we'd be borrowing Vicky's ride. But now we had our own! Valla's father's car was amazing. And it has a big back seat! Mmmm... We were pelted with rice, that I knew I'd compulsively clean up every grain when we returned, as we got into the car and drove off toward our honeymoon. Valla coughed.

I'll spare you the details, but what occurred those next two days is forever burned into my memory, I gladly make space in my endless compulsive loop area for it. I thought I had known passion with Valla before this, but knowing we belonged to each other as a married couple multiplied things tenfold. We were asked by the hotel staff on more than one occasion to keep the noise level down. I take pride in that, and in making Valla walk funny for a week. Though I didn't fare any better. Swoon!

Chapter 15 – Family

We had a scare after our honeymoon. A virus had made its way past Valla's weakened immune system. The resulting pneumonia and associated kidney problems put her in the clinic for two days. With a week of prescribed bed rest and another round of drugs.

Vicky and I kept her current on her coursework so she wouldn't have to stress over catching up. I suffered two episodes that week I was so stressed over the reality of Valla's condition. Thankfully one was at home and the other was in my art class, but Jenny calmly led me to her private office to weather it away from of the prying eyes of my classmates.

This health scare brought something boiling to the surface in me that had been at the back of my mind for months. I wanted a child... not just that... I wanted a child with Valla. Not because it was on her list (although that would happily cross out the third item from her list of four) but because I loved her so much and I wanted to make a new little life with her. The reality of her condition made this a real priority for me.

She was afraid but she really wanted a child, so I convinced her but under the condition that our child wouldn't be at risk of suffering Valla's affliction. We discussed it at length and researched the hell out of it. I wanted her to donate the eggs and we'd find a clinic with anonymous sperm donors for the other raw material, and I would carry our child.

The more I learned about her disease, the more I despised it. I was shocked at how many people suffer the affliction and how little press is given to the subject. It scared the heck out of me. It saddened me learning the facts of the terminal nature.

In most cases, it wasn't the disease that killed but the effects of it weakening the immune system. If you didn't die of eventual excruciatingly painful suffocation, it was usually pneumonia, liver failure, or kidney disease that took the victims. I spent time hiding in the garage crying for my wife after learning this.

But I also learned that as long as the sperm donor was screened for the cystic fibrosis gene there was zero chance of our child suffering from the affliction. And even if the donor had the gene there was still only a 50/50 chance of the child suffering from the disease.

The procedure was expensive but didn't even dent Valla's and my funds. Between her inheritance, the art commission money, and Valla's book that would be published in the summer (Under the name Vee A. Jacobs thank you very much) we had over three million in the coffers and growing. That fact shocked the heck out of me since I didn't pay attention to it, Vicky did all of our finances, I just handed her the checks.

Within weeks, Valla's eggs were harvested we had 'the' appointment. That was pretty damn uncomfortable, let me tell you, and it was not guaranteed that it would be successful. But then days later, happy days of happy days, I missed my period!

The three of us were gathered by the sink in the master bathroom, jockeying for position around the little white stick that would determine our fate. We didn't bother with a timer as they knew I was counting in my head. “It's time,” I whispered and reached for it, turning it over. As one we leaned in to look closer... PLUS!

I went deaf for a moment as Vicky squealed in one of my ears and Valla squealed in the other. I stood there stunned. I'm going to be a mommy! Finally I looked into Valla's eyes. “We're going to be mommies,” I whispered. There was a flash as Vicky took a picture of Valla and I kissing over the pregnancy test. That girl and her cameras.

Weeks rolled by, school ended and summer floated by. We found that we would have a daughter, which elicited more excited squeals from us all. Valla's condition was slowly degenerating, spurring more frequent trips to the clinic as I was getting bigger. She religiously wrote in her leather bound books. Our commissions and publications kept us busy when we weren't doing it like bunnies in every room of the house. Being pregnant made me so, I still hate the word but, horny!

The new school year started and Oxford was really fighting hard to get Vicky now. What school wouldn't want to tout someone with perfect grades and an IQ off the charts on their rosters? Offers of them funding her graduate and post-graduate work were dangled in front of her like a carrot. Which, by the way, made Vicky say she'd make an awesome bunny! But she slapped them down yet again.

The first kick was another life-defining moment for us. I squealed out loud and moments later the girls came running in panic into the garage. They looked to where I sat on my stool in front of my easel, working with my hand on my belly.

“What is it!?! What's wrong!?” Valla was yelling with Vicky standing beside her looking concerned. I grabbed each of their hands and placed them on my belly as the baby kicked again.

Vicky squealed and Valla laid her head on my belly and started crying. Her sobs shaking me as I leaned down to lay my head on her back and we both cried. Vicky stroking our hair making shushing sounds. It was real, this IS going to happen. Against all odds, Valla would be a mother before she was taken from us.

Mid December rolled around and I felt fat. I was huge! How could Valla love me? I'm so rolly polly! Like a platypus who ate a watermelon. I can't wait to get this child out of me! The nursery had been ready forever, Vicky and Valla had spent months on it. And I had done a mural on the ceiling with hundreds of stars from the night sky how they would look on her birthday, made with tens of thousands of tiny dots of glow in the dark paint.

I was standing in the nursery watching my two girls moving the crib around... again, when... “Oh.” I stood there a second then uttered, “Baby?” Valla and Vicky were arguing about optimal sunlight through the window for the baby. “Valla?” I said louder.

They were pushing the crib again. “VALHALLA ABBEY JACOBS!” I yelled and the two girls froze and looked over at me finally.

I glanced at my feet, their eyes followed to the wet floor. My water had broken.

“Holy shit!” Vicky chirped.

“It's time.” Valla mouthed in awe and shock. The next moment, all around chaos ensued.

Vicky was grabbing my overnight bag from beside the changing station then grabbed all of our purses, repeating, “Oh my God! Oh my God!” over and over again. Valla looked panicked, not knowing what to do or how to help.

“The car,” I whispered to her, breaking her out of it. She ran into the garage, then seconds later ran back in and over to Vicky to get the car keys, then went sprinting back into the garage. I was still standing there when Valla came running back in looking sheepish and grabbed my hand gently to lead me out, patting my pocket to check for Little Vee.

Now, I seriously don't recommend having a baby for sport. It is no fun in any way shape nor form. I still wonder how I was able to push my daughter out of me, thinking of how apt that lame old analogy of a watermelon through a garden hose seemed at that time.

Just like a bad cliché I must have told Valla a dozen times how much I hated her for doing this to me during the contractions, only to cry about how much I loved her seconds later. My emotions were everywhere, and this hurt!

But then it was over. I heard my daughter cry for the first time and everything in life was simply perfect. When the nurses were done checking her out, weighing and measuring her, and putting a cute little pink cap on her, they handed her to Valla. I saw the most beautiful sight I had ever seen at that very moment, even more beautiful than my wife.

It was the woman I loved crying tears of joy as she held our child whispering, “Welcome to the world Abbey Victoria Jacobs, we've been waiting for you our entire lives.” I seared that moment into my memory, taking in every tiny detail.

She walked over to me with the biggest smile I had ever seen on her face and gently passed Abbey to me. “Look, Abbey, here's Mommy,” she whispered. Then Valla stroked my hair while staring at our baby. She glanced at me with an adoring smile. “You did good Mia!”

I reached my lips up and kissed her, not able to take my eyes off of Abbey. “Oh my God Valla... we're a family!” I said matter of factly just as a squealing blondie came bounding into the room, followed by a smiling Mr. and Mrs. D.

Chapter 16 – Storm on the Horizon

This is the year I refer to as our best year, our perfect year. The one quality year we had before Valla's health took a turn. I cherish every family outing, every hour playing with our daughter, every minute together, every moment we stole away to make love, every millisecond I could keep Valla smiling.

I marveled at the way Valla smiled at Abby or myself with such love in her twinkling eyes. I lived a lifetime in each of these moments. Cherishing them. Returning that love every chance I got.

The only dark spot that year was just before the start of Junior year, when Oxford had finally won Vicky over. We saw her off at the airport, and so many tears were shed. Watching her walking up the concourse through security, then turning to wave in tears was the last time Valla would ever see our friend and the second to last time I would.

She wound up finding love and a wonderful, spectacular life in England. Sure we still send occasional emails from time to time, and Christmas and birthday cards each year... well-intentioned promises are always made to visit some time but never followed through. An amazing, fitting, present comes every year for Abbey's birthday, tons of thought obviously put into each. But her departure truly was the end of an era.

We had to scale way back on the commissions we took. We spent most of the time we were not in class with our amazing baby and ourselves. She was our gift from God, our greatest accomplishment. This caused demand for our works to spike, driving perceived values through the roof. We still stayed at the top of our class with our grades and Valla still religiously wrote in her leather bound books.

Then that storm on the horizon finally caught up with that one perfect year. Half way through our junior year Valla had a cold. Then I got a call from our babysitter that Valla had shown up at home after her classes but had collapsed. She had already called an ambulance and told them which clinic to bring her to.

Valla had gotten a bad infection from her cold which had damaged her already weakened kidneys. They had to hook her up for dialysis. Something that would become a weekly ritual from that point on. To my dismay, we learned that she was not qualified to go onto the transplant list because of her condition, so we had to live with it.

Her health was spiraling out of control. We hired in-house care to help out when she wasn't in class. But we somehow made it through our junior year. We visited the beach frequently that summer, where Valla could lay on the sand with Abbey and relax and just enjoyed being with us.

Crowds gathered there once as I used a stick to poke thousands of holes in the wet sand as the tide went out to make a picture of Abbey. Embarrassing me but making Valla beam at me with pride. I basked in it.

I had frequent breakdowns in the garage, I wouldn't ever let my Valla see my weakness. I would be strong for her... for us, for our child.

So many whispered I love you's were shared between us, our hands always interlaced when we were near each other. We made sure to always be touching in some manner.

Our senior year finally began. Valla had more determination than any other student, she would finish college, she would get her degree, for her father, for herself. NOTHING would stop her, especially not this damn disease! For a time, she got a little better, and we spent more time going out doing things as a family while we could. We even got a couple 'dates' squeezed in. But then after Christmas, her health started deteriorating quickly again.

By May she couldn't attend class anymore, she was confined to in-home bed rest but her mind was still sharp as a razor. The instructors allowed me to bring her assignments to her for her to complete at home. I hated seeing the woman I loved looking so frail. She would still transfer all of her poems to her handwritten books.

Abbey had started speaking, calling us Mommy and Mama to our tears of delight.

Then in June Valla's liver began to fail, the clinic insisted on 24-hour care and we had to move her into a hospice. They said that she was alive through sheer force of will alone at this point. Valla was irate. “Two weeks! Just two more fucking weeks! I'm going to graduate, they can't do this to me! I won't let it win!” she spat out.

I spent the day calming her and letting her know I'd figure it out. “I love you so much Valhalla, I won't let it beat you... beat us. You are so strong and so beautiful. Give me a day to get this worked out.” She kissed me more passionately than she had been able to the past six months. It was the perfect kiss. I can still feel it today.

I had spent time with all of her professors the next day. They all agreed to give her her final exams early, that she could do them at the hospice. I had never seen a person with more fire, more determination than the love of my life over the next two days as she chewed up those finals and spit them out. Receiving almost perfect scores, making them her bitch!

She rested the next week, sleeping and gathering her strength. We convinced the staff to allow her to attend the graduation in a wheelchair against medical advice. When her name was called and I wheeled her out to receive her diploma where she got a standing ovation. I was bursting with pride for my girl. Just how awesome is she?

I leaned in to kiss her on the lips then she whispered, “I told you I'd do it, love, I completed my list.”

I whispered back, “I had no doubt, baby. I love you so much and I am so very proud of you!” She smiled a genuine one hundred percent Valla smile that made me go weak in the knees, “I love you too my Mia.”

Three days later Valla woke up in the hospice as I sat by her side with Abbey on my lap gnawing on Little Vee and she grabbed my hand, interlacing our fingers. I looked into my wife's twinkling eyes as she spoke, her voice was stronger and clearer than it had been in a long time. “Mia. I want you to promise me that you will keep doing your art when I'm gone... and to make sure Abbey has a happy life.” She paused for me, I nodded my head then she continued. “YOU are my greatest accomplishment, I don't know how I was lucky enough to find you, to find love... but you gave me the strength to live a lifetime in your eyes, to do what I set out to accomplish. Every day was a gift, and I'm glad I filled those days with you. I'm so completely in love with you.”

I answered in a whisper, my breathing was ragged, “I have ALWAYS loved you Valhalla.”

She whispered, “It was worth every moment.” She smiled at me and closed her eyes for the last time. I lost the love of my life and I cried silently over her until the nurses led me away.

Chapter 17 – A New Purpose

I hadn't slept or eaten since then. The next evening I was still numb, sitting at home, hiding in my hoodie. I was lost planning Valla's funeral when suddenly I heard the front door lock open. I jumped out of my chair at the sound. A moment later, a frantic and disheveled looking Vicky was running in, her eyes sweeping the room till she saw me and wordlessly ran over to me and grabbed me in a protective hug. I buried my head in her shoulder as we slid to the floor, and finally my heart-rending sobs came.

Between sobs and gasps for breath after a while I whimpered, “She's gone.” She just lowered my hood and stroked my hair and let me cry myself to sleep in her arms. An hour later I woke to the sound of Abbey crying in the nursery, I went to get up out of Vicky's arms and she stopped me.

“No, I'll do it. You need to sleep.” She helped me up and led me to my room first. The room I used to share with my wife, my Valhalla, where she sat me on the bed before she left to go to the nursery.

I was counting... when she returned twenty-two minutes and thirteen seconds later, I was sitting in the same place on the bed. She undressed me, throwing the hoodie out into the hall roughly like it was poison and put me in my sleeping clothes, pressed Little Vee into my hand, then helped me under the covers. I held the covers open and she didn't hesitate to slide in behind me and wrap her arm around me protectively as I fell asleep crying into my pillow.

When I woke up the next morning grasping Little Vee, I felt more human... human, with a large hole torn in my soul, but human. I looked back and Vicky was awake already, in the same spot as last night; protecting me, watching me.

"Hey," she said with a little smile.

I whispered back, "Hey back. You're here? I thought I dreamed it."

She nodded. "I hopped a plane in London the moment I heard. I'm so sorry Mia."

I fought the tears off. She stroked my hair. "I wanted to make sure you were awake before I went to take care of Abbey. I didn't want you to wake to the empty bed and think I had left. I'll be right here. You rest and I'll be back soon. I'm going to change and feed Abbey then make you some breakfast. Then I'll take care of everything... I may have some questions, but I'm here for you," she said rapid fired to me at hyper speed.

I reached a hand to rest on her cheek, I'd never been happier to see her and her ability to take charge of chaos than at that moment.

"Victoria... slow down. Breathe."

She smiled at me and slid out from behind me and started toward the door, turning and calling over her shoulder, "Get some rest, Mia."

Thirty-six minutes and fifty-three seconds later she was back in the room holding a tray with oatmeal, toast, and coffee. I started scarfing down the food. I didn't realize how hungry I was, I hadn't eaten since before... I stopped for a moment. "Two thousand two hundred and eighty minutes and seven seconds," I whispered. Then I started drinking the coffee as I blankly stared off into space.

Vicky looked at me, squinting her eyes as I saw her calculating in her lightning fast brain. "Stop," she said.

I whispered, "That's how long I have been without her."

She looked at me and said more firmly, "Stop!" She shook her head and forcefully continued, "Don't do that to yourself, Mia!"

"I can't do this. I can't go on without her," I said flatly with no emotion. And for the second time in my life I was slapped. I actually lost track of my counting and stared at her in shock.

She looked mad, something you don't see on Vicky's face, ever... it wasn't flattering. She spoke firmly between her gritted teeth, "You are stronger than this! Don't let it beat you, don't let it define you! You are one of the strongest people I have ever met and Vee made you that much stronger! What would she tell you right now?! Huh?!"

I stared at her. She's right... Vicky is always right. Valla made me strong. She made me promise to give Abbey a happy life. Half of my heart is gone, but the other half is still here, beating strong. I'll make Valla proud of me, no matter how bad my heart aches for her! That's my new purpose. I'll define myself with Abbey, I'll fill my days giving her the best life I can! I can burden this pain that I will always have.

I looked at her in embarrassment. “Sorry Vic... thank you.”

She smiled one of her contagious smiles. “No problem Mia.” She took a deep breath, “That was the easy part. You ready for the hard part now?”

I nodded, absently rubbing Little Vee with my thumb. I could do anything, Valla taught me that. I stood up and hugged the little blonde Einstein, and she led me out to the living room to the mountain of paperwork and legal mumbo jumbo.

It was astounding all of the things that needed to be done. Things I would never have imagined. But Vicky was a machine, she handled everything as easily as we breathe. Every once in a while she asked a question and once I answered she'd be filling out forms, making calls, sending emails, kicking ass, and taking names.

Mr. and Mrs. Davenport had arrived, hugging me before springing into action. Maira went into autopilot and took care of Abbey. Mr. Davenport gave legal, technical, and moral support to his daughter as she plowed through everything. I had forgotten that Frank Davenport was a high-class lawyer with clients like that Mandy Fay Harris singer. I felt useless.

More than once the phone rang and I heard Vicky hissing something I couldn't make out. Once Mr. Davenport intercepted the phone and was walking outside with it. I could hear his raised voice outside, “Don't you vultures ever stop? You will not make a circus out of this girl's tragedy!”

I learned later that news and 'entertainment' reporters were trying to get an interview with me about my wife's death since we were both making a name for ourselves in the art world. Vicky had been skillfully parrying them away. From this point on, Mr. D manned the house phone.

At one point, he came to me with a pained look on his face. “The paper wants to know if you want to submit an obituary or if you want them to write it.”

This struck me hard, silent tears made their way down my cheek, but I refused to cry out loud. “V-Vicky already h-has it. S-sh-she can email it t-to them.” I raised my chin to try to show strength. He rested his hand on my shoulder gently then put the phone back to his ear and wandered off relaying the instructions.

The service was that Saturday at our house. Vicky would be with me for only one more week before she had to return to England. I looked out from the house to the back yard. There were chairs arranged around the yard at the dock. About a dozen people showed up that we had approved. I pulled on Valla's combat boots and wandered out with Valla's ashes in an ornate porcelain urn.

I looked around as I stepped up to the dock and placed the urn on the little lace covered table there. Jenny was there as well as Valla's English Lit professor. The Davenports, of course, Maira holding Abbey on her hip. The Cohans and their current foster child, Danny. Dr. Townsend and two of the nurses from the hospice, Nancy, and Grace.

Then there was Missy... again, who stood and walked over and gave me a warm heartfelt hug conveying real sympathy. “I'm sorry Mia,” she whispered so nobody could hear her, before returning to her seat. I was stunned, in all the years she had made my life a living hell in school she had never used my real name.

Vicky looked over to me, so I nodded and spoke to the gathering, “Th-thank y-you all for coming t-today. Valla would h-have appreciated it, and I a-appreciate it more th-than I can express in words. We are h-here to celebrate Valla, not mourn her passing.” I was gaining courage just speaking about the love of my life. “She was the miracle I needed, my savior from a world I h-hid from. She showed me what it was to love and be loved. Every day s-she demonstrated what true courage and strength was. She taught that lesson to me and instilled it into me and anyone who she took into our inner circle of friends and family.”

I was smiling in memory now. “Valla beat all odds, in a cruel world stacked against her. She accomplished EVERYTHING she set out to do. Naysayers and her godforsaken disease be damned! She found love, got married, built a family, and had a beautiful daughter with me. And her last fate-defying act against the universe was to graduate from college, even if it meant doing it from a hospital bed and a wheelchair.”

I was swelling with pride for my wife's accomplishments. “She showed us all what true strength was. She once told me that every day is a gift and what we do with that gift is what defines us. I lived a lifetime with her in the four years she gifted me. I am defined by the love we shared and by our daughter, whom I'll spend each and every day sharing that love with.”

I turned and opened the urn and walked along the dock, sprinkling her ashes into the lake she grew up on. At the home, she created a family with me. I felt a semblance of peace for the first time since her passing.

Vicky and I caught up over the next few days before she left. She had met a wonderful woman who she thought might just be her Valla. And because of her impeccable record and demonstrated management and organization skills she had been offered a curator position at a high-end art gallery while she does her post-grad studies at Oxford. Large businesses were already taking note of her reputation.

She says I inspired her to find something in business and the arts, so when she was offered the position she thought, “I would so make an awesome curator!” And like everything else she sets her mind to I had zero doubt that she'd be amazing at it.

She slowly helped me put myself back together enough that I could survive on my own. Then I watched her leave for that final time at the airport, each of us whispering our “I love you's” through our tears.

Epilogue

Mia looked at Abbey and Samantha with tears in their eyes as they were clearing away the dishes of the dinner they ate during the story after they had moved from the living room as the story progressed. “So... incredibly long story short, that's the story of your Mother and I. Why did you want me to tell it?” Mia finished.

Abbey wiped the tears from her eyes and looked up with the coy look on her face that Mia remembered from her wife whenever she was up to mischief.

“Well Mom, I was wondering the exact moment you fell in love with Mother.”

Mia smiled in memory again, “That's easy. It was right after she slapped me and said 'Every day is a gift! It's how you fill that gift that defines you.'... why do you want to know?”

Abbey turned to Sam, biting her lower lip seductively. “You remember on the plane ride over when you asked me when I knew you were the one? And I changed the subject?”

Samantha laughed at that. “Well if you call sticking your tongue down my throat 'changing the subject,' then yes I remember.”

Abbey continued, “Well before I answered I wanted you to hear that story.”

The realization was spreading across Samantha's face and she whispered, “No fucking way!” Abbey was nodding and looking at

Sam with hunger in her eyes. “Yes. It was that night of our second date in our freshman year. Do you remember what you said to me?”

Sam nodded in amazement. “I said that every day is a gift and that I wanted to fill all my days with you.” Abbey was nodding like a mad woman. “Yes. That was the moment that I knew you were the one.”

Mia was stunned at this revelation as she watched her daughter slyly distract her girlfriend with a seductive kiss on the lips as she pulled a little box out of her pocket.

Samantha's hand shot up to her mouth when Abbey took a knee and opened the box. “Samantha Prudence Roth... will you make me the happiest woman alive and marry me?”

Sam was just nodding up and down quickly, repeatedly, her hand still on her mouth and a tear in the corner of her eye.

Abbey laughed. “Is that a yes?”

Sam dropped her hand then pulled Abbey into a passionate kiss, then broke it quickly, reaching her hand out for the ring. “Yes! A thousand times yes!”

Abby slid the plain band etched with intertwining script S's and A's onto her fiancee's finger. Then they held hands, fingers laced and turned to a smiling and crying Mia.

“I love you girls so much!” she exclaimed and pulled them both into a hug. She was about to suggest they celebrate when her cell phone vibrated in her pocket. She looked at it. “Drat! It's the curator bugging me about getting the exhibit there tonight. Can you girls lend me a hand?"

They nodded and she looked at the text again.

[Missy: Hey freak, u getting yr crap here or not?]

She typed a reply, [Mia: chill skank, b there soon]. Mia slipped on the old worn combat boots by the garage door that had been repaired and resoled multiple times over the years before heading into the garage.

As they loaded the art into the racks in the old FJ Cruiser, Sam asked Mia, "So, you've never found anyone else in all these years?"

Mia shook her head. "No, I've never found anyone else attractive since Valla, I've resigned myself to the fact that she was a once in a lifetime lightning strike for me. But the years I had with her were more than enough to fill a lifetime with love." Sam nodded with a sad smile as they all piled in for the ride to the gallery.

Abbey and Sam took the back seat so they could steal glances and kisses that they didn't think Mia could see. Their hands always together, fingers laced. Abbey asked, "So why the night delivery? The exhibit doesn't open until tomorrow night. What's the rush."

Mia shrugged with a quizzical look on her face as she concentrated on driving. "Don't know. The curator was babbling something about the new owner of the gallery wanting to meet me as soon as possible. Probably some old blowhard that wouldn't know art if it jumped up and bit him."

They arrived at the back of the gallery. Mia tapped the horn and as the big bay door opened she drove in and the door closed behind them. They got out and were in the process of unloading the canvases when a middle-aged woman with grey streaked hair in a smart business suit came quickly walking over to them. “You finally made it spaz!”

Mia smiled at the woman as they shared a quick hug. “What's the rush whore?”

The two younger girls were looking between Mia and the other woman in confusion. The older women's actions toward each other belied the crude verbal sparring they were engaged in.

Mia noticed their confusion and chuckled at them. “Girls, this is Missy Hannigan, the curator here.” The girls looked shocked at that revelation that this was Mia's childhood nemesis standing in front of them. “Missy this is...”

She was cut off by Missy's exclamation, “Jesus Christ!” She was looking at Abbey, a hand shooting up to cover her mouth, then whispered over toward Mia without breaking eye contact with Abbey. “She looks EXACTLY like her.”

Mia smiled with pride at that fact and continued like nothing had happened. “This is my daughter Abbey and her gorgeous fiancee, Samantha.”

Missy shook each of their hands with a smile. “Pleased to meet you both.” Then she turned to Mia. “You did good for a freak.” Nodding her head toward Abbey.

Mia beamed. "That means a lot coming from you bitch." The younger girls still looked stunned about who this was, the story fresh in their heads.

They unloaded the canvases and put them on the dolly Missy indicated to them. Missy stood back and looked at the works, then whistled. "You definitely haven't lost your touch spaz." Then Mia turned to Missy, sighing and resigning herself to the next task at hand. "So where is this old windbag who wants to meet me?"

Missy smirked at that comment. "Follow me."

Mia knew that smirk... Missy was up to something.

They were lead into the gallery proper and Missy pointed to the far end, where Mia's exhibit would be tomorrow. "I'll catch you tomorrow freak."

Mia nodded as she lead the girls over to a tiny woman in a gorgeous, professional black dress, with her back to them, examining the plexiglass shelves which would hold Mia's canvases.

Mia cleared her throat and steeled herself for the inane questions that were sure to follow. "T-the curator s-said you'd like t-to speak with me."

The stunning woman spun around quickly, with a big infectious smile. "Is that all you have to say to me, Mia?"

Both women squealed and jumped into an embrace. Mia squeaked out in excitement, "I can't believe you are here!" The blonde looked over Mia's shoulder as they hugged, then gasped and quickly broke the hug, taking two steps back in shock and covering her mouth in surprise.

Then just as quickly she tilted her head toward Abbey in question, searching Mia's eyes. “Abbey?” Mia was just grinning like an idiot and nodding, feeling an odd fluttering in her stomach that felt familiar somehow when she looked at her old friend. The blonde dropped her hand from her mouth, shaking her head slowly. “I thought I saw a ghost.”

Mia grabbed both of the woman's hands interlacing their fingers, pulling her to the girls, but unable to pull her gaze from the short, gorgeous blonde who looked ten years younger and fitter than her forty years should show. Vicky was similarly appraising Mia, her eyes stopping first at the familiar combat boots, then at Little Vee's ears poking out of her pocket. She smiled genuinely at both.

Then Mia realized she was staring at the blonde and quickly picked the conversation back up as she spoke with pride. “Victoria, let me introduce to you, your god daughter Abbey and her beautiful fiancee Samantha.” Now it was the girls' turn to cover their mouths in shock at hearing the blonde woman's name, as Vicky gave them exuberant hugs then grabbed Mia's hands again.

“Where's your bride?” Mia inquired, looking around in curiosity but not releasing her hold on Vicky's hands.

Vicky was subconsciously stroking the sides of Mia's thumbs with her own thumbs, a fact that Abbey and Samantha didn't miss. Vicky shrugged, “Who knows? She divorced me two years back, bilked me for millions in the settlement. Said I was too hyper for her, and age wasn't mellowing and 'maturing' me enough for her tastes. I personally think it's because her personal assistant knocked her up. Tomato, tomoto... But I so make an awesome divorcee!" She finished exuberantly and struck an exaggerated, coy pose that heated Mia's cheeks. Everyone laughed at Vic's revelation, it was such a Vicky thing to say.

Then the blonde babbled out at superhuman speeds, "I got bored over the pond. Running large businesses on your own is like, so lame. When I heard a few months back that the prior owner of this gallery was selling I jumped at the chance to come home again. I've always had a soft spot for the arts, and I figured I'd make a friggin' amazing gallery owner, so I bought it. I arrived here last night and am livin' outta a hotel till I get settled. Now I'm here for good. I heard you were turning down galleries left and right, but approved mine and..."

Mia had a permanent smile plastered on her face now as she interrupted, "Slow down Vickster! Breathe!" The younger girls were outright laughing at the exchange now. Mia was reveling in the contact of her hands with Vicky's. She knew this flushed, tingly feeling from somewhere.

Mia offered, "Well, welcome home! You simply must come stay at the house tonight so we can chat! We can get your stuff out of that stuffy hotel tomorrow. You are staying with us until you get situated!"

Their eyes met, and both women bit their lower lips, staring hungrily at the other. This was not lost on either of the young girls as they mouthed "Oh my God!" to each other excitedly.

"Definitely! I've missed you so much!" Vicky said.

Mia smiled in relief. "Great! So we'll see you at home soon!" She leaned in to kiss Vicky on the cheek, but she stopped short when she finally realized what she was feeling. Could it be true? Mia pulled slightly back and locked eyes with Vicky again, asking silent permission. When Vicky's eyes flickered down to Mia's lips and she leaned slightly forward, Mia closed the gap and they came together in a passionate kiss. The familiar sensual merging and sliding of their lipstick leaving each of them craving more.

Abbey and Sam each had their hands pressed together against their lips like a silent prayer as happy tears started flowing down their cheeks while they watched as lightning struck twice.

The End

Romance Novels by Erik Schubach

Books in the Music of the Soul universe...
(All books are standalone and can be read in any order)
Music of the Soul
A Deafening Whisper
Dating Game
Karaoke Queen
Silent Bob
Five Feet or Less
Broken Song
Syncopated Rhythm
Progeny
Girl Next Door
Lightning Strikes Twice
June
Dead Shot

Music of the Soul Shorts...
(All short stories are standalone and can be read in any order)
Misadventures of Victoria Davenport: Operation Matchmaker
Wallflower
Accidental Date
Holiday Morsels
What Happened In Vegas?

Books in the London Harmony series...
(All books are standalone and can be read in any order)
Water Gypsy
Feel the Beat
Roctoberfest
Small Fry
Doghouse
Minuette
Squid Hugs
The Pike
Flotilla

Books in the Pike series...
(All books are standalone and can be read in any order)
Ships In The Night
Right To Remain Silent
Evermore

Books in the Flotilla series...
(All books are standalone and can be read in any order)
Making Waves
Keeping Time
The Temp

Books in the Unleashed series...

Case of the Collie Flour
Case of the Hot Dog
Case of the Gold Retriever
Case of the Great Danish

Novels by Erik Schubach

Books in the Techromancy Scrolls series...
Adept
Soras
Masquerade
Westlands
Avalon (2018)

Books in the Urban Fairytales series...
Red Hood: The Hunt
Snow: The White Crow
Ella: Cinders and Ash
Rose: Briar's Thorn
Let Down Your Hair
Hair of Gold: Just Right
The Hood of Locksley
Beauty In the Beast
No Place Like Home
Shadow Of The Hook (2018)

Books in the New Sentinels series...
Djinn: Cursed
Raven Maid: Out of the Darkness
Fate: No Strings Attached
Open Seas: Just Add Water
Ghost-ish: Lazarus

Books in the Drakon series...
Awakening
Dragonfall

Books in the Valkyrie Chronicles series...
Return of the Asgard
Bloodlines
Folkvangr
Seventy Two Hours
Titans

Books in the Tales From Olympus series...
Gods Reunited
Alfheim (2018)

Books in the Bridge series...
Trolls
Traitor
Unbroken

Books in the Fracture series...
Divergence

Novellas by Erik Schubach

The Hollow

Novellas in the Paranormals series...
Fleas
This Sucks
Jinx (2018)

Novellas in the Fixit Adventures...
Fixit
Glitch
Vashon
Descent (2018)

Novellas in the Emily Monroe Is Not The Chosen One series...
Night Shift
Unchosen (2018)

Short Stories by Erik Schubach

(These short stories span many different genres)

A Little Favor
Lost in the Woods
MUB
Mirror Mirror On The Wall
Oops!
Rift Jumpers: Faster Than Light
Scythe
Snack Run
Something Pretty
Summer Break (2018)

www.ingramcontent.com/pod-product-compliance
Ingram Content Group UK Ltd.
Pitfield, Milton Keynes, MK11 3LW, UK
UKHW020142250726
13967UKWH00002B/820